MW00526247

A CIGARETTE
LIT BACKWARDS

A CIGARETTE LIT BACKWARDS

TEA HACIC-VLAHOVIC

THE OVERLOOK PRESS, NEW YORK

This edition first published in hardcover in 2022 by
The Overlook Press, an imprint of ABRAMS
195 Broadway, 9th floor
New York, NY 10007
www.overlookpress.com

Library of Congress Control Number: 2022933605

Printed and bound in the United States

1 3 5 7 9 10 8 6 4 2

ISBN: 978-1-4197-6289-5
eISBN: 978-1-64700-733-1

ABRAMS The Art of Books
195 Broadway, New York, NY 10007
abramsbooks.com

For Stefano

In loving memory of

Giancarlo DiTrapano

&

Joshua Parsons

Hello world, I'm your wild girl

—The Runaways

DEXTER'S LAB

Everyone knows Iggy Pop and the Stooges lived in the Fun House, right? Even Nico stayed there, cooked badly, and gave Iggy an STD. The place was legendary, and our scene had the same thing. Dexter's Lab was our Fun House. A spot between Carrboro Elementary and the train tracks. Fridays after school I'd take the bus downtown and walk twenty minutes to get there. I wasn't allowed at Dexter's on school nights.

"'Sup, Kat?" Dexter loomed in the doorway.

"'Sup, Dexter." I squeezed past him, holding my breath.

Dexter stalked me down the hall and his stink followed. In spite of his stench, he was lethally hot. Or because of it. I only held my breath to spare myself from his powers. Dexter's BO was a fatally poisonous aroma. His sweat a seductive secretion that caught girls like bugs in a Venus flytrap. Deadly Dexter. His grin was feral and snaggle-toothed and mauled everyone he saw. A smile from Dexter was a punch in the gut with brass knuckles. His exquisitely greasy hair could oil a thousand cast-iron skillets.

I barely resisted grabbing it as I gazed up at him. He towered over me, at six feet. His body was frail and his complexion ghostly. He wore the same outfit each day. Like a cartoon character, he had a uniform.

Crusty blue jeans with tapered calves and tears in the knees. Ratty British-flag sweater held together with safety pins. Silver pyramid belt and steel-toe combat boots. To top it off, a work of art: his classic black leather biker jacket was painted, patched, studded, and spiked to perfection. It held so many trinkets I couldn't count them if I tried. They were meticulously placed and so beautifully arranged, I was astounded he did it himself. But I wouldn't dare question it. In our scene, boys embellished their own threads. DIY fashion was honorable. Sewing was masculine. Chances were Dexter didn't change his underwear, either.

Only Ashley saw Dexter's underwear. She was his girlfriend and I hated her for that. She was the prettiest punk in our scene and probably the whole country. She could have been on *America's Next Top Model.* I told her that once and she said reality TV is for sellouts. Ashley was nearly as tall as Dexter. Her limbs were long and lean, and she flailed them around when she talked. And she talked all the time. Ashley always had something cool, funny, or loud to say. Everyone listened. Ashley took up space and demanded attention. We were all stuck on her. Ashley's hair was fire-red and spiked. She had two things most teens didn't: body ink and face metal. The cherry on her shoulder was an homage to Cherie Currie. A silver ring squeezed her bottom lip, accenting its plumpness. There was something obscene about it, like her mouth was a glazed Krispy Kreme donut pumped full of strawberry jam. Her face was a southern gothic masterpiece, with swamp-green eyes and sky-high cheekbones. All her outfits were sick. Nylon pants, fur coats, sequin tops, latex boots, heart-shaped glasses . . . nobody knew where she shopped. She didn't like me but she didn't fight me. She barely acknowledged me, actually. She knew I didn't steal people's boyfriends.

I stomped over smashed beer cans, slimy pizza boxes, and crumpled cigarette packs on the way to the fridge door. How'd he do it? Nature's meth: teenage rage. Dexter replaced a regular door with a refrigerator door. So there was a refrigerator door in the middle of the hallway. When you opened it up you didn't see the inside of a fridge.

You'd see the Party Room. The fridge was smaller than a regular door, so you had to duck to go inside. The door was elevated, so you had to jump into the room. *Alice in Wonderland* meets *Trainspotting*. Because of this ducking and jumping, not even the coolest person could make a smooth entrance into the Party Room. Some tried but it was impossible. I liked this because I was the least cool person in our group. The fridge gave everyone a bad shot. I followed Dexter inside, trying not to stare at his butt crack, which always peeked out of his pants. It winked at me and I blushed.

"Guys, Kat." Dexter introduced me to grown-ups sprinkled around the Party Room. "Kat, guys." You can be a grown-up without being an adult. Being an adult means you have an adult life. These were just kids who "grew up" physically but were still like us inside. I nodded at the trailer park dealers and they nodded back. When everyone was done nodding I found a relatively clean spot on the carpet to sit down on. I crossed my legs and pulled my coat over my outfit. I hated my clothes.

I shopped at the PTA thrift store. Used tennis skirts, worn men's jeans, and yellowed wifebeaters made up my wardrobe. Plus precious shirts I copped at concerts. I had a Casualties shirt, an Anti-Flag shirt, a Bouncing Souls shirt, and a Blink-182 shirt I couldn't wear anymore because when I did my friends called me a "poseur." (When that happened, I had to wear my shirt inside out.) My favorite jeans were too big for me so I closed them with a safety pin. One day the pants were on my floor and the safety pin was left opened and I was reaching over my bed to turn over my Specials record and I tripped and stepped straight onto the needle. It went through my foot and I had to get a tetanus shot.

Dexter's Lab was always full. Kids came from Chapel Hill High (old public school), East Chapel Hill High (new public school), Carolina Friends (private school for hippies and reluctant children of hippies), and Village Charter (sketchy strip-mall institution for pregnant teens and fuckups). A couple of kids were dropouts, like Dexter. He was eighteen when I met him but by then he'd already lived alone. There were rumors, of course. Like, he emancipated himself from his abusive parents and hustled for a living.

Or, he was orphaned and tossed between foster homes until he ran away and squatted in an abandoned building (which became his Lab). The most believable theory was that his grandma raised him and Dexter inherited her place when she died. The worst rumor (told by the worst people) was that he killed his parents to turn their home into a party palace. "Their bodies are still hidden somewhere." I couldn't believe anyone would joke about that. Dexter was sweet. And I knew a hint others didn't.

Months ago I'd gone into Dexter's bedroom to leave my coat on his bed, but the bed was full of other people's coats, and I was worried something would happen to my coat, since it was my dad's. So I thought I'd hang it in Dexter's closet. In his closet I saw a uniform, similar to what Dad wore to work. It was hanging there, in his size, with his smell. So he must work at a garage. He fixed cars or bikes . . . otherwise he was a plumber or handyman, all those uniforms look alike. Anyway, I figured when all of us went to school or wherever, Dexter went to work. He didn't talk about it, because I guess he didn't want to spoil our fun. Nobody likes crushing a rumor.

Sometimes a little kid from Culbreth Middle School hung out. He was a miniature Rude Boy. We called him Little Tim. He was only twelve but freakishly tough. Nobody messed with him. The boys would say, "He's a baby, I'll smack him when he's in high school." The truth was even the rowdiest guys were afraid of him. He was like that Chucky doll. Tiny and terrifying. Sometimes deadbeat grown-ups dropped in to sell weed or booze. They'd usually only hang out long enough to make out with some punk girl. They didn't try with me. I guess I looked younger than sixteen. I wasn't allowed to dye my hair or get piercings. My boobs weren't in yet. My haircut was the same home-cut bob I'd had as a kid. The color? Forgettable. My scalp didn't have the balls to produce a strong saturation.

"Is there beer?" I asked Dexter.

"PBR." He pointed to the kitchen.

"Get me one!" barked Little Tim.

I crawled to the fridge door and hopped into the hallway. Then I headed to the real refrigerator. Aside from booze the fridge offered a jar of pickles, a few bottles of hot sauce, and an oily bag of biscuits from Sunrise Biscuit Kitchen. That was Dexter's favorite food. He revealed this to me once, during a rare moment alone with him. I was honored to learn a secret about him, or even a widely known fact, so long as he told *me* privately. That night, he held a biscuit out toward me.

"I get extra for mooches."

"No, thanks."

"You anorexic? Or racist?"

"I prefer grilled cheese. It's my favorite."

"David Lynch's favorite sandwich is the grilled cheese." He unwrapped the foil to reveal a cold biscuit, moist with condensation.

"How do you know?"

"He said so." He ripped into it.

"On MTV?"

"In a magazine." He talked with his mouth full.

"You read magazines?"

"Yeah, when I wipe my ass with them." He laughed and spit a crumb on my lip. I didn't move it. That crumb could live on me forever if it pleased.

"Hah. Good one."

"Anyway, if your favorite sandwich is grilled cheese that means you're classic, like Lynch." Dexter presented this information to me as a fact. Then he scarfed the rest of his biscuit and washed it down with sweet tea. It didn't seem very cool to be considered "classic." I didn't want him to think that of me.

I clarified, "That's not my favorite *sandwich*, that's my favorite *food*."

"What's the difference?" Dexter burped.

"If that were my favorite *sandwich* it would imply I have other favorite kinds of foods, that I eat an ambitious selection of food. But grilled cheese is my favorite food, period. It's all I wanna eat." The conversation ended there, as it did whenever I talked too much. He shrugged, turned, and zipped into the Party Room, leaving me alone in the kitchen. I shuddered at the memory. Most of my memories had that effect. Especially those in which I'm talking to a guy.

But this was a new night, a new opportunity to not suck. I grabbed two beers and darted back into the Party Room. Real smooth, I tossed Little Tim his beer. It fell on the floor and rolled to his feet.

"Nice one, Kat. Now it's gonna explode."

I sighed, walked over to Tim, bent down, picked up the beer I threw, and gave him the other one. As I did so, my whole body burned with shame. *Everyone's watching you. Everyone hates you.* I rushed back to the safety of my spot and tapped the dropped can.

Nice one, Kat.

"Are y'all going to the Trippy Dope show?" I squeaked.

Trippy Dope was equal parts rock star and wild animal. Raw force. He was always half-naked. Onstage he rolled around on broken glass and bled everywhere. Trippy Dope was the genius of our generation. Our generation's Bowie. Our Mozart. I'd never forget when I first saw him. I was watching *TRL* on MTV, well, half watching it, talking on the phone with my friend Lucy. We always watched *TRL* on the phone together after school. We'd make fun of whatever *NSYNC or Eminem were doing while crushing on Carson Daly. It was fun, kid stuff. Then Trippy changed the game.

Trippy Dope's debut music video for "Too Bad Too Good" premiered in 2001.

Lucy and I stopped talking, we were rendered speechless. It was a simple video, no special effects or backup dancers. None of that teenybopper crap or faux pop-punk. He sang his track while walking down a dark highway, barefoot and topless. Headlights illuminated his features. Each passing car revealed a different, harrowing, striking face. He was pure, he was true, he was the real deal. The way he moved his body shook something in me. In my underpants, sure, but also spiritually. His voice cracked my skull open and curb-stomped my heart.

By the end of the video, I was desperately in love (and had hung up on Lucy). By that night on Dexter's floor, I had both his albums and every magazine he graced. I fantasized about him daily. I dreamed of meeting him somewhere, not at his shows, not as a fan. That he'd see me sitting at a bus stop and notice me. He'd catch something special about me. *This is crazy, I don't know you, but, will you be my muse?* That daydream was dangerous to indulge in. Snapping out of it broke my heart. Trippy Dope was my God.

"He's gay," Dexter coughed through smoke.

"He's a pussy," Little Tim shouted.

"I wanna fuck him," Ashley growled. Dexter threw her a dirty look and she stuck her tongue out at him. He pretended to punch her in the head.

"If there's nothing else to do," a dealer grunted.

"Let's all go together?" Nobody heard me or maybe they did but didn't answer me so I pretended I didn't say anything. I looked around as if I was really interested in and focused on something across the room.

The Party Room was deformed, like part of it shrank and part of it swelled up in some freak accident. The colors were moldy-green and barfy-brown and dried blood–red. It reeked terribly, like something was rotting. I longed to spend more time there but I was too busy maintaining my lifestyle and responsibilities. My parents only let me hang out (on weekends) if I got good grades. I was prepping to audition at a music academy in Winston-Salem. I had community service, since I got caught buying Adderall at school. On top of all that, I had to nurture my crushes and trick them into thinking I was cool.

ELMO'S DINER

Elmo's had the best grilled cheese sandwiches. The bread was buttery and crisp around the edges but soft in the middle. The crusts were firm but flaky and slightly burned. The cheese was rich and melty but held itself together just long enough to make a stretchy scene when you tore the bread apart. Every sandwich was presliced in half, on a diagonal. It came with a juicy pickle and a cup of coleslaw. I dipped each bite into slippery ketchup. Heinz only. My parents forced me to eat other stuff sometimes but I preferred not to.

When you move to Winston-Salem you'll be famous at every diner. "Here comes Kat, the best piano player in town . . . she's awesome . . . we're so lucky she moved here." You'll float down the street, surrounded by friends . . . you won't miss Chapel Hill. You'll visit sometimes, only to see shows. By then you'll be so cool you'll go through pains to hide your boredom of what once thrilled you. "There goes Kat . . . if only we'd appreciated her when we had her." Frat boys kicked me out of my daydream by bumping into my table and spilling coffee all over my lap.

"Sorry kid, I didn't see you."

"I didn't see *you* either," I sneered, cleaning the mess.

I paid my bill and walked to the bookstore. It was Saturday, community service day. Before finding Independent Books, I had all kinds of service jobs. I worked at an animal shelter, a nursing home, highway cleanup, juvie jury duty, focus groups, catering . . . I was thirteen when I got in trouble so this felt like a life sentence.

My luck was I got caught the first time I tried doing anything harder than weed. The bitch Spanish teacher watched me copping the pills in the cafeteria. She didn't stop me in the act, she let me go through with it *and then* pulled me into the office. So she could incriminate me. Cold. They called the cops and everything. They wanted me to write a report and narc all my friends out. I refused and broke down crying. Not being a snitch is harder than it looks.

The principal put the pills in a ziplock bag and gave them to the cops. They were like, it's probably ecstasy, we've got to test it. Even though I told them a million times they were just hyper meds. I was kind of relieved they took them out of my hands. I had an excuse not to try any drugs for another semester.

"Please don't call my mom *please*. Call my *dad*," I begged the principal. I thought Dad would care less. I thought he wouldn't understand because he didn't speak great English. He did understand, and the way he looked at me was haunting. If he was mad, he hid it from me. Mom did, too. They weren't mean because they were worried. And probably in denial. During my Teen Court trial they told the judge what a "good kid" I was. The judge was like, "I didn't ask for a statement." They bought me new piano books for the two weeks I was suspended from school. It was like a holiday. When I came back to class everyone treated me really special. But that only lasted a few days, until a popular girl shot herself in the head in the bathroom.

Independent Books was my favorite gig. The store was my playground. My coworkers were dust and mice. I just sat around reading magazines. I didn't touch the books because they were all hippie propaganda. I hadn't figured out how to work the register because while my boss taught me I wasn't paying attention because he made me nervous because he was cute. So I pretended to know and now I'd never know. Sometimes I asked the customers for help. Once I gave a book away for free because they were so frustrated with me. Luckily we only got like one customer per day. Nobody read radical stuff around there. Nobody who could pay for it, at least. I didn't worry about being fired because you can't fire someone who works for free.

They carried a new underground magazine called *Vice*. It was like *Punk* magazine for Y2K. I loved the "Do's and Don'ts" section. This writer commented on pictures of people taken around the world and decided whether the people pictured were a "Do" or a "Don't" based on their outfit and attitude. If they were a "Don't" he was really brutal. The "Do's" were mostly hot girls with boobs. Sometimes I wondered if I would be a "Do" or a "Don't" but tried not to because I knew what the answer was. Every week I flipped through the same issue of *Fruits*. I memorized each page of Tokyo street kids. I'd never seen anything like them. Even Ashley didn't look that cool. We stocked some porno as well. My favorite was a black-and-white magazine called *Smut*. I tried not to look at it too often because it made me feel funny and when I felt funny I had to go across the street.

One of my crushes lived across the street, at Chapel Hill Comics. He didn't live there, he worked there, but it's like, when you only see your teachers at school you assume that's their home? Bob was a grad student at UNC. He had a radio show on the student radio where he played experimental electronic music. I thought he was cool though I doubt his peers agreed. My friends wouldn't have thought he was cool because he wasn't punk. He didn't fit into any scene. He was weird and gawky and dressed dorky and knew everything about comics. His hair was thin and his glasses were thick. My crush on him burned strong. He tolerated me.

"Hey, Bob." The door went ding-dong when I stepped in. I waved and walked to a bin of comics. I always flipped through that bin first. There was never anything new.

"How's the community service?" Bob teased me from the register.

"Serving the community." Flip, flip. "Got anything for me?"

"Only superhero stuff."

"Hmmmmm." I sighed and moved to the next bin. Flip, flip, flop.

"Your Clowes should arrive next week. There's some gruesome manga coming in as well." He changed the music to something dark and robotic.

"Are you going to the Trippy Dope show?"

"Nah, fuck that guy. He's a creep."

Flip, flip, flip. "I'm going."

"I know, Kat. You go to every show." Bob winked at me then turned away to help a customer. He really knew how to work a register.

SCHOOLKIDS RECORDS

Technically I was a poseur. One day back in the sixth grade I saw Max wearing a Bouncing Souls T-shirt. The shirt was black and THE BOUNCING SOULS was written in a font made of white ghosts. It was sick. Max was my crush at the time and he was the biggest punk in middle school (at the time) and I knew that he knew what was cool. I'd never heard of that band before. I wasn't even sure it was a band. You couldn't just go around asking people what bands they liked because they'd know you wanna steal their tastes. And you definitely couldn't point to their shirt and ask, "Is that a band?" because then you were dead meat.

So after school that day I walked to SchoolKids Records and searched through the "B" bands and sure enough, the Bouncing Souls did exist. I chose their *Hopeless Romantic* album and shoplifted it. I ran home hoping it was worth it, praying it was good. In my room I fervently tore the packaging off and slammed the disc in my boom box. "Hopeless Romantic" is the first track on the album. It changed my life.

I decided to become a punk. I did everything a punk did: I hung out with punks, dressed as punky as I could, went to every show, drank beer, disobeyed authority . . . but ultimately the way it all started couldn't change. It was my secret to live with forever. What did matter was I loved the music. It was made for me. Punk rock is pure, it stands for nothing.

Monday after school I took the city bus downtown. My lunch money burned in my pocket. I walked by the regulars: the cart lady, the guy with baby doll heads stuck all over his car, Crazy Pete, the crackhead who bought me beer at the gas station . . . we all acknowledged each other. I liked living in a small town because if you walked around enough you could become a local celebrity. I knew that when I moved to Winston-Salem I'd have to start over but I didn't plan on staying anonymous.

The sickest job anyone could have was at a record store. It didn't matter who you were or what you looked like. If you worked at a record store, you were the shit. Forever. The guys at SchoolKids knew me because I was in all the time. Sometimes I bought stuff and sometimes I shoplifted. They didn't suspect anything. I walked up to the cashier and pressed the little bell, the ones hotel lobbies have, even though he was standing right there. "Seriously?" He hated that. He was a BMX biker so he always wore cutoff jean shorts to show off his leg muscles and calf tattoos. White ankle socks peeked out of his low-top Chucks. A bandana hung out of his back pocket. Stringy hair was slicked backwards, with gel and sweat, reaching the collar of his dirty white shirt. He smelled like Old Spice deodorant. I knew because that's what I used, since Dad bought them in bulk. I stared at him and forgot to talk.

"What's up, Kat?"

"Huh? Oh. Can I get a Trippy Dope ticket?"

"How old are you?"

"What?"

"Are you old enough to get a Trippy Dope ticket?"

"Yeah, of course."

"Can I see ID?"

"Uhhhhh," I made a big scene of digging through my tote bag. Comic book, duct-tape wallet, disposable camera, tweezers, lip gloss, flip phone . . . I looked up at him, pleading with my eyes. No sympathy was given. "Crap. I forgot it at home . . . be back later." I shuffled toward the door when he started cackling.

"I'm messing with you."

I turned on my heel. "Huh?"

"It's an all-ages show."

"Asshole."

I handed him the dough and he passed me the ticket.

CAT'S CRADLE PRESENTS
SATURDAY JAN. 17TH 8:30 PM
TRIPPY DOPE ***W/SPECIAL GUESTS***
***** $18 ADVANCE TICKET *****
300 E. MAIN ST. CARRBORO ***967-9053***

I stuck it into my *Ghost World* comic and dipped out. As I bounced down Estes Drive I fantasized about the show and all of the scenarios that could happen to me there. *Stardom, adoration, a synchronized dance sequence, kissing Dexter, making Ashley cry* . . . I relished the impossible scenes deeply. Daydreams were my specialty. I could walk for hours and not even notice, so long as I had a compelling scene on rotation in my brain. As Blondie said, "dreaming is free."

I was always home alone. Never did I have to sit through family dinners or crappy TV. All immigrant parents work late. My mom was a research scientist, and my dad was a mechanic. Ex-Yugos are always scientists or engineers. Dad was gonna be an engineer but then he knocked Mom up.

My parents didn't know anything about my social life except that it was no good.

They thought my friends were lowlifes. I wondered how low I could go.

I took my clothes off in my parents' bathroom. I looked at myself naked in the mirror. My body was like a boy's body but softer. *One day you'll look in the mirror and like it. Any minute now . . . Until then try not to kill yourself.* I didn't have any grand idea of how I should look. I wasn't obsessed or anything. I just knew a better version of me was supposed to show up a while ago. I got my period at eleven, earlier than Lucy or the other girls. I thought that was a good omen, like I was destined for greatness. That year I'd wake up each morning, excited like on Christmas. I'd run to the mirror to see what was new. Eventually I stopped. The early period was a fluke. At sixteen I looked like a taller version of that sixth grader. I didn't wake up excited anymore, just resolved. I'd take waking up as a cockroach, like Kafka. At least that would show progress.

I showered and changed into pajamas. Then I went downstairs and microwaved a cup of hot chocolate. I took the cup to the piano and set it on the top. I got comfy on the bench and started my scales. I was memorizing Beethoven's Piano Sonata No. 14 in C-sharp Minor, op. 27, no. 2, also known as the Moonlight Sonata. Moonlight is a good song to impress people with because everyone's heard it in some movie. I wasn't an amateur, though. I was only memorizing Moonlight to pull the heartstrings of whichever sucker would judge my audition. I was also learning Beethoven's Sonata No. 15 in D Major, op. 28, and Chopin's Waltz in D-flat Major, op. 64, no. 1, known as the *Minute Waltz*. I had it down to six minutes. Only Chopin could play it in a minute, legend has it. The really great contemporary pianists could play it in about two and a half minutes. Chopin would love punk rock because the best songs are the shortest.

I had a love affair with Bach in the eighth grade. He was a bad boy. He made each hand do unrelated things. Psychotic. I got a body high playing his two-part inventions all day. Affairs like that can't last long, you need someone more reliable and less intense. Not that I would have known. I'd never had a real boyfriend.

Max and I made out at Timberlyne Cinemas when I was twelve. We were friends already but something about that invite, "You and me, Friday night?," screamed: this is a date. *My first date*. I wore a black tank top with a lightning bolt on it and tight jeans with studs on the side. Both from Limited Too, a dirty secret. He wore his freshest skater threads and a face doused in aftershave, even though he didn't shave. The film was scary but scarier even was his kissing. I'll never forget the sloppy Frenching. My mouth was a dance floor for slugs.

At thirteen I went to third base at the skate park with a bunch of skaters . . . but that wasn't up to me.

Summer after middle school I had a fling in Surf City. On my way to Island Delights I spotted an adorable boy on a balcony. He was peeling potatoes. The flakes fell on me like snow. I looked up and laughed. He looked down and said, "Wait." He walked me to the diner and we shared a grilled cheese. He was a sixteen-year-old metalhead with curly hair. We kissed in the ocean that night, in our underwear.

Spring of freshman year I dated Grear. We met in front of Cat's Cradle. He was waiting in line to buy tickets for a show. His friend already had a ticket. I had my own ticket . . . until I gave it away. "No way, it's sold out." Grear looked crushed. He was gorgeous and I had no choice.

"Have mine."

"What?"

"Have my ticket. Go in with your friend."

"Are you serious?"

"Yeah." I held it out.

"Do you want money?"

"No I'm good."

"Are you sure?"

"I've seen Bright Eyes before."

"You're amazing. Thank you."

I walked around aimlessly until it was late enough to call Mom for a believable pickup. I hadn't seen Bright Eyes before. I couldn't wait to see him. I felt like a dumbass, until I got a voice mail the next day.

"Hey, Kat? This is Grear, from the Cradle. You gave me your ticket and I got your number from a friend. Let's hang out?"

Over coffee he told me he was into photography and went to Durham Academy. I'd never met a private school kid. Friends School didn't count, that was for kids with no future. Durham Academy molded the future Assholes of America. He was pretty normal, I guess, but after I found that out about him I couldn't help but think about it. PRIVATE SCHOOL hung over his head in a neon sign. We only kissed a few times in the daytime before he took me to Chelsea Theater. *Cowboy Bebop: The Movie* was playing and I was dying to see it. What I did see I didn't enjoy because I was paralyzed with nerves. Finally Grear grabbed my hand and rubbed it over his jeans. The denim was stiff and warm.

When we made out he felt me up and discovered I was wearing a push-up. Since that night he never called me again and I never wore a bra again.

Summer before sophomore year I met Josh at Southpoint Mall. That was the turning point of my life. More important than watching Trippy Dope for the first time. Meeting Josh was destiny. Everything that happened to me until then led me to that moment, in that mall. After meeting Josh I knew I'd never be the same. I was fifteen and he was seventeen. He was sitting at the fountain by Southpoint Cinemas, smoking a cigarette.

"What's up, sugar pie?" His southern accent was a sparkling swimming pool full of maple syrup. I fell into it like quicksand. "Wanna hit?" A fountain angel came to life and offered a cigarette. By the first puff I was addicted.

Josh had shoulder-length black hair and diamond-blue eyes. He wore baggy torn jeans and an oversized Misfits shirt. He must have spotted my outfit and knew I'd be cool. That's what I liked most about being punk; it was easy to spot allies and be recognized as one. We shot the shit for a couple of hours. He really got me and I got him. By the time Mom came to pick me up, I was wrecked at the thought of leaving.

Ruthlessly torn away. Josh and I were stuck together, irreversibly, like bubble gum on a shoe. I was the bubble gum.

When I asked for his number he insisted, "Gimme yours, I hop around." He was one of those kids whose parents didn't care if he ever came home. Sometimes he slept over at my place, on the sofa downstairs. Those mornings, Dad would take Josh to McDonald's. The thought of them nibbling McMuffins side by side in Dad's pickup truck delighted me. Dad's garage was by Southpoint, so he'd drop Josh off there on his way.

"Where is Josh school?" Dad asked. "I say to him, I drive you to school tell me where is. He say man don't worry. Mall good I take bus."

"Yeah, his school is in Durham near the mall," I lied.

Josh didn't go to school. He hung around the mall all day until he could go home with someone. When he wasn't with me, we'd talk on the phone. He called me from pay phones, café phones, stranger's phones, and phones of friends. He didn't have his own cell. I had to wait for him to call. It was romantic in an old-fashioned way. Gut-crushing in an old-fashioned way. Like war. Josh played piano. He didn't own one but he played mine better than I did. Every time I asked him where he learned, he'd tell me a different ludicrous story. We'd talk about music for hours. Classical, jazz, and his compositions. I never wrote my own music. I did once, and my piano teacher said it reminded him of Evanescence. Never again.

Josh would go on about this girl, Sarah. He said he was in love with her and sometimes asked me advice about her . . . I kept it up to keep him on the phone. He kept saying (threatening) he'd hop a train to Mississippi and "get her back." The harder I fell for him the less I could bear it. Hearing her name was a stab in the heart. If it went on this way I'd die.

He called me on my sixteenth birthday, and I confessed my feelings. I don't remember quite what I said but I'll never forget how he answered. "You know I love you, Kat, but not like that." Then he disappeared. Was he with Sarah? I still jumped every time the phone rang, hoping it was him. It never was, so I talked to him in my head. At night I dreamed about him.

Ceaselessly I obsessed over screwing everything up. I pushed him away. Boys don't react well to feelings. I should have shown my love physically. If I were experienced, if I were a *real girl*, if I had some *balls*, I would have snuck downstairs those nights he slept on my couch and made love to him silently. Instead I stayed awake, wide-eyed, waiting for him to creep up to me. How could he? My parents slept next door. What an idiot. I missed my shot.

I had to lose my virginity to avoid messing up with the next boy. The plan was I'd do it with Bob. Then, maybe I'd "grow up" and get a real boyfriend. My goal was to do it by Valentine's Day. I bought my Trippy Dope ticket on Monday, January fifth. So I had time. I planned it all:

I walk into Chapel Hill Comics and say,

"I rented that anime you told me about. But I don't have a TV in my room."

"We can watch it at my place," Bob replies.

That night I come over. I'm wearing a red dress I don't own yet. His house is small and comfortable. Stacks of books are piled high, a sofa is smothered in pillows. His fridge is full of beer because he's old enough to buy it. We sit next to each other and watch anime. I have a couple of beers, to relax. He kisses me first. I kiss him back, which he takes as a sign to undress me. He does everything while I lie there because he knows what he's doing and knows that I don't. Afterward, we finish the movie. It isn't weird between us because we know we can't be a couple, because of the age difference.

From then on when I'm in the store everything is the same, except for our secret. It's undetectable by anyone except us. We feel it as a low energy, a soft bass line beating underground. A stylish, adult connection.

I got the *Minute Waltz* down to five minutes and forty six seconds. I chugged my hot chocolate and started again, from the top.

EAST CHAPEL HILL HIGH

Riding the school bus was good for my image. My friends teased me for living in an "actual house" on the good side of town. One day Charlie came over to take a leak and he said, "You're rich." He lived in public housing with his dad. It was embarrassing. I didn't invite anyone over anymore.

I took the bus to school in the morning, and I took it home in the afternoon. I sat in the back and listened to music. I tried to stay out of people's drama. The other kids who took the bus were always yelling and hitting each other. They left me alone because they knew who my friends were.

At lunch the punks sat outside on the hill and nobody ate. They didn't have lunch money and their parents didn't pack them anything. The preppy kids drove off campus to eat at Bojangles, a southern fast-food chain specializing in sweet tea, fried chicken, and biscuits. Coming back to sixth period with a Bojangles cup in your hand was a status symbol. Mom used to pack my lunch. I convinced her to give me lunch money, which I pocketed for concert tickets and CDs.

Freshman year sucked because my middle school friends went to a different high school than I did, on the "bad" side of town. I didn't know anyone and Ashley scared me so one day I sat down at a table full of nerds playing Dungeons & Dragons. One of the nerds was cute, though he didn't know it. Lat had long, gold hair and wore plain clothes. On him they looked fashionable, because he was naturally skinny and pretty, like an elf from *Lord of the Rings*. I was crazy about him. Each Saturday fall semester I went to his place to play Dungeons & Dragons. Lat was the Dungeon Master and his friends were elves and wizards. I'd come over early and be like, "I need you to explain the rules to me again," thinking, *I'm here to make out with you*. But he never got the picture and eventually Charlie transferred to my school. Charlie was a godsend. He told Ashley I was cool. So I started sitting on the hill with them and high school became bearable. Lat and I still said hi in the hallway, but he didn't know why I abandoned the dungeon.

Charlie and Ashley weren't the only punks at East. Madeline was a poseur. I remember what she was like in middle school. She listened to Britney Spears and wore Abercrombie & Fitch. Then she started dating Max. One weekend she bought a whole new wardrobe at Hot Topic. She didn't even cut her hair or do her makeup differently. My friends thought I was well-off but she was actually rich, like, her parents went to restaurants and took vacations. I saw her get into her dad's BMW once after school. She saw that I saw her do it but I didn't tell anyone.

Madeline was American Girl Pretty. She had natural blonde hair and freckles and a straight smile from wearing braces. Of course she wasn't as pretty as Ashley, her boss. Ashley wasn't the boss of me because that would require her to consider me a friend and call me outside of school and look at me without disdain.

Nosebleed was the opposite of Madeline. He came out of the womb with a mohawk, which he glued every morning. He wore bondage pants and denim vests with spikes every day. We called him Nosebleed because he got a nosebleed at a show once and sprayed the blood all over the skinheads. His real name was Joseph. I talked to him a bunch but didn't know him, really. He only answered questions with one or two words. Like, "Right. Rad. Huh. Yep. Totally. I guess." His favorite thing to say was "I guess." He said it about a hundred times a day . . . *I guess*. Nobody knew if it was all an act or his actual personality. Nosebleed would have made a great boyfriend because he was polite and knew how to drive.

Lucy wasn't punk anymore. She became a stranger. We were kids together and, more important, immigrants together. From different countries but the same in that our houses were too weird to invite Americans to. I made that mistake once and sent a girl home in tears. Because all we had for dinner was sausage and sauerkraut and my parents' friends were drunk and yelling "in foreign" and we watched an R-rated movie with nudity. I always felt too loud and strange in American-girl houses, but I didn't cry about it like they did at mine. To me it was bizarre how their psycho moms programmed every minute of a sleepover, with extravagant snacks, planned activities, and church on Sunday. At least my parents let us chill and watch TV and go outside and open the fridge whenever we wanted to make ourselves a Pop-Tart.

I saw Lucy walk by and she looked away and I felt that poke in my stomach. I couldn't see her without seeing everything at once. The violet headband she wore in first grade. Her thick, black hair. Her parents singing karaoke. Boiled chicken legs. Funfetti cake and scary movies. Wendy's Frosties. Her mom's dumplings. Watching her sleep in her sleeping bag. Her boobs when they just started growing and she didn't wear a bra.

Crystal dragon statues and barrels of rice. Homemade soy milk. Her handwritten notes. Her screaming "Kat, help" when her dad kicked her on the lawn.

"Kat?" Charlie pulled at my pigtail. "What's with you?"

"Huh? Nothing."

"Want a hit of this?" He offered me his joint. I hated smoking during school.

"Oh, sure." I closed my eyes and sucked in.

Charlie put his arm around me. I hoped everyone could see. Charlie was king. He was equally charming and rough. Everybody respected him. As the only Black punk in our scene, he had to become extra bad to put up with the bullshit. His hair was dyed in a leopard print. He skateboarded well and fought like a pro. He enjoyed teasing me, saying he liked how "innocent" I was, which I hated. I didn't want to be innocent, but I also didn't want him to stop liking that about me. He held my hand sometimes, in the hallway. One night last fall, he was Mad Dog drunk and joked about wanting to be my boyfriend. He was rolling around in the Party Room, like, "Kat's too good for me, I can't touch her." Everyone laughed because Charlie had real girlfriends, with tattoos.

"Johnny Rotten was a poseur. Johnny Thunders hated him."

"Shut up, C-Rock. The Pistols invented punk."

"Ashley, are you stupid? It started at CBGB's with the Ramones."

"Well, the English punks were more hard-core."

"They didn't even shoot up until the Americans came. Everything they did was a copy of what they *thought* went on in New York. Come on, Meg. Don't be a Nancy."

"Nancy was an icon."

Charlie and Ashley fought and I watched. I wasn't sure whose side I was on. I preferred the New York Dolls to the Sex Pistols. But I loved the Clash more than Television. I didn't see why it mattered where a band was from or who started what. When do people decide their opinions are worth arguing about?

"Nancy was a nutjob crack-hoe bitch. She ruined Sid Vicious. Who was a closeted homo, by the way."

"Fuck you, C-Rock." Ashley walked away and Charlie walked me to class.

"See you Friday, Kit Kat?"

"What's on Friday?"

"Party at Dexter's Lab."

"There's always a party at Dexter's."

"This one's a *real* party." He pecked me on the mouth and strutted off, ditching class.

I took my seat and zoned out. Did Charlie just kiss me? I couldn't concentrate or see the whiteboard. I kept forgetting to tell Mom that I needed glasses. School desks were torture for the left-handed. So were notebooks with spirals. So was writing with a pen because my hands were always sweaty. The sides of my palms were permanently black. I did the bare minimum to make my parents happy. Most schoolwork came naturally but it still felt like torture. Teachers often told me that if I "applied" myself more I could get into Ivy League schools. So I applied myself less. My uncle tutored me in precalc once and said I could be a mathematician if I wanted. Who would *want* that? I tried to deflect his compliments. "Math isn't real but death is. And I'm bored to death."

I used to help a hippie in my class with his math because he fried his brain with pot. He only understood stuff when you explained it to him a hundred times. We had to meet in secret because my friends always said, "Never trust a hippie." Ashley caught me with him once and I had to lie about what we were doing together. Was it worse to hang out with a hippie or tutor math? I convinced her I was buying weed from him. So she told me to bring the weed to Dexter's that weekend. So I didn't go out that weekend. And I stopped tutoring the kid and for all I know he dropped out.

When I got out of class, Charlie was waiting.

He said, "Let's ditch the rest of the day."

It didn't feel right to ditch. I began to shake my head and think up a bogus reason why I couldn't leave.

Before I could, he said, "We'll go to Dexter's."

I couldn't snub that.

We took the city bus to Franklin Street and from there we walked to Dexter's. He held my hand the whole way. His hands were big and warm and calloused. I worried about mine sweating but he told me not to.

PTA THRIFT SHOP

I needed an outfit for Friday nobody had seen me in a million times. Punks didn't change their clothes much. Hygiene wasn't our priority. Punk boys could wear the same threads all week. Punk girls couldn't, but they could get away with more than preppy girls could. At East, preppy girls never repeated the same outfit or even a *part* of an outfit in one week. What a life. Punk girls were freer, we could get away with two or three outfits per week, mixing the combinations, so it didn't look like we were repeating. If a punk girl wore the same exact outfit two days in a row, or more, she'd say "I stayed out all night" or "My parents kicked me out" and that would be cool. Ashley was an exception, as she was for everything. She wore incredible ensembles each day. I couldn't recall ever seeing her repeat an outfit.

Punks only changed jackets and shoes seasonally. Combat boots in the winter, Chuck Taylors or skate shoes the rest of the year. Only Nosebleed wore boots year-round. A leather biker jacket was standard most months. In the winter everyone added a hoodie underneath. Nobody wore puffers or pea coats. In the winter we were all freezing. I alternated between a lime-green raincoat and Dad's moto jacket. It wasn't a biker jacket in the Hells Angels or Ramones way. It was European, a Ducati white and red leather jacket worn by racers in the seventies. Dad used to wear it on his bike. When I was little, I'd ride with him, from behind. But we fell once, and Mom got scared and didn't let me go again. Our garage always had several bikes in it that Dad was "fixing" to sell. Then he'd end up riding them and not selling them. The Ducati was too big for me, my fingertips barely poked out of the sleeves.

Charlie and Ashley saw me every day, so I tried to avoid wearing school looks on weekends. My showstoppers were my tennis skirts: I had a violet one and a red one. They were deadly short. I got them both at the PTA. I wore both skirts that week already. I headed to the PTA to try to find something new. Fat chance.

The PTA could be gloomy or great, depending on context. If you had to go there with your parents it was miserable. Once you went on your own, it was fun. I hit the men's section first. Mom once asked me if I was a lesbian because I looked at men's clothes every time we went into a store. This was when I was thirteen and wanted to be a boy. I mean, I didn't want to have a dick or anything. I didn't want to be a girl, it seemed like a drag. Freud's "penis envy" is a stupid concept. Little girls don't envy penises; they're objectively ugly. We envy the power that people with penises have. At least I did.

The way I saw it, girls sucked in movies and they sucked in comic books. Girls sucked in songs. They were never the protagonist of anything unless they were hot. Girls weren't on MTV's *Jackass*. They didn't get to make people laugh by kicking themselves in the balls. I couldn't picture myself becoming a hot girl, so I decided not to be one at all. I skateboarded and hung out with the skate boys. I wasn't any good but they didn't make fun of me. I had a sick World Industries deck with Flame Boy and Wet Willie. I wore Airwalks and baggy cargo pants. We'd meet up every weekend at the park, skate around for a bit then smoke weed in the woods. When we got munchies we'd hop over to 7-Eleven and demolish all the junk food in sight.

Everything was perfect. Until girls who didn't skate started showing up to the park. One of them was dating an older skater. The girls who didn't date anyone just hung around, gawking at the boys. My boys called the girls "Betties." The following weekend the boys gave me an ultimatum. They were like, "Betties are hanging out at the park now and they wanna hook up. So if you're gonna hang around us you have to give it up." I didn't say anything, so they all pounced on me. One held me down while the other two stuck their tongues in my mouth and their hands under my clothes. When it was over they were like, "What's wrong?"

After that happened I hung around them more than ever. I guess I needed to make the whole thing "worth it" to myself. To remind myself that I wasn't just some dumb chick, I was their friend. So I'd let them take turns feeling me up. Under my shirt or in my pants. That pair of jeans with the studs on them that I wore to the first date with Max? They ripped in one leg, on the upper thigh, when I started growing out of them. The boys would stick their fingers up the hole in my jeans to reach my underwear. They'd touch me in the parking lot before school, at lunch, between classes, whenever they wanted. I was a walking target. I kept telling myself, *It's cool, you're their friend.*

But they didn't treat me like a friend anymore. It was all physical. And a couple of them got girlfriends, whom they treated nicely. I wasn't a friend or a girlfriend, I was something in between. Something unsavory.

I stopped going to the park and I started being a girl. I figured, if that kind of stuff will happen to me anyway, I may as well make it happen myself. I may as well be somebody's girlfriend. I had Dad take the trucks off my deck.

In the PTA changing room I tried on: men's plaid pants . . . too Insane Clown Posse. Girl's flares . . . too Christina Aguilera. A black baby doll dress . . . too Kittie. Everything was terrible. I realized I'd have to resort to cutting. I blasted Minor Threat as I marched home, wondering whom to sacrifice.

You can't make something out of nothing but you can make new clothes out of old clothes with a pair of scissors. Jeans into jean shorts, a dress into a skirt, a dad's button-down into a gown. I threw all my clothes on the floor and started digging.

Obviously, I couldn't cut my tennis skirts. They couldn't get any shorter. I already cropped and cut the sleeves off most of my punk shirts. If I did anything to my jackets my parents would kill me.

I plucked an ancient Gap dress out from a tumbleweed of forgotten items. *Meet your new fate, bitch.* Mom got it for me, for one of my recitals. It was a black satin A-line, too long and classy. Could I turn elegant into hard-core?

I cut upward into the hem with the scissors, about an inch. Then I tore it into a minidress with my hands. Satin rips easily. I used the scissors to slash holes and gapes and slits all around. Voilà: a party dress. I laid her on the floor with some fishnet tights, my Dr. Martens, and Dad's coat. The perfect look for a teenage runaway.

I always laid out my outfits for the next day on the floor. I made a figure out of the clothes, starting with the socks and shoes at the bottom, then the pants or skirt, the top, the jacket, accessories. Sometimes I spent hours arranging looks and changing my mind in the middle of the night and having to turn the lights on and do it all over again. Sometimes I fell asleep on the floor.

PARTY ROOM

I heard Dexter's Lab from across the street. The sidewalk vibrated. Bass pulsed through the bricks. Hoots and hollers shattered the windows. The whole building was a throbbing stereo. I knocked on the door and nobody answered. I rang the doorbell and nothing. I kicked the door, stupidly. After a couple of minutes I twisted the doorknob and let myself in.

The Lab was chaos. Every punk rocker in North Carolina was crammed in one spot. How did they organize themselves? Like a million rats, scurrying out from gutters, trash cans, and pipes, taking twisted routes until meeting in a filthy abyss. For real, most of them didn't have cell phones. Did they use snail mail? Messenger pigeons? The answer was MySpace. Everyone had it but me. It was new, not even the preps at school caught on—but scenesters and punks were hooked. They could share music, promote bands, local scenes, and the hierarchies within their scenes. I was all for it, for their sake. But I'd never get one. The crew kept bugging me about it so I lied and said Mom found my page and made me delete it. "You could make another," Nosebleed said. I shook my head. "She watches me like a hawk." I could have ten MySpace pages if I wanted. The truth was I didn't want an internet presence. This socializing website was set up for trouble. It bred competition. The thought of having to publicly display a selection of my "top" eight friends? Or have to claw my way into someone else's top eight? The politics filled me with angst. Being scrutinized in person was bad enough—publishing pictures of myself online to be judged by my friends seemed like a nightmare. Anyway, they all connected on MySpace and good for them. I'll admit it was inspiring to witness these messy people get their shit together for a party.

If someone wanted to wipe out all the punks in the state, they'd merely need to bomb Dexter's Lab. I wasn't kidding, we had them all: the Asheville anarcho punks, Wilmington skate punks, Boone crust punks, Durham oi! punks, Charlotte straight-edge punks, Fayetteville street punks, Cary folk punks, Greensboro glam punks, Winston-Salem art punks, and Raleigh SHARPS (skinheads against racial prejudice). Some random train hoppers, too. Everyone from out of town seemed hard-core, more legit than we were. What did they consider us? Mall punks? I shuddered at the thought.

One thing they all had in common: the dudes were hot and the chicks were scary. Nearly everyone was coupled off. Stephanie and Sid were the only duo more famous than Ashley and Dexter. They rarely hung out at the Lab because they lived in Raleigh. Their presence meant the night was special.

Lots of rumors spread about them, but here were the facts: Stephanie was only thirteen when she started dating Sid, who was twenty-four at the time. When she lost her virginity to him he gave her herpes. Then, Madeline drove Stephanie all the way to Tennessee to get an abortion. I knew that was true because Madeline had Polaroid pictures to prove it. Stephanie's mom kicked her out when she found out, so she moved in with Sid. Imagine, getting to live with your boyfriend. Stephanie knew we talked about her and held her head with dignity. That marvelous head. Her skull was a perfect sphere, on display with a "Chelsea" cut: completely shaved aside from bangs and sideburns. Nobody else had the balls to pull that off. She was hot in a different way than Ashley was. Stephanie wore men's clothes, mostly from Sid's closet. But she didn't look butch. Hiding her "jailbait" body under gross boy threads drove everyone raving mad. As if what she had underneath was so powerful she was saving us the burden of seeing it.

Sid was a dick. He fronted a (locally) popular ska band and thought of himself as a god. During the day he did construction. Not bad, since Dickies overalls and CAT boots fit his aesthetic. I squeezed past him and he elbowed me. I barely got from the hallway into the Party Room alive. There was no space to move or breathe. Like a mosh pit, without the band. Without the point.

The Party Room was packed but I spotted my crew. Dexter was throwing pills at Ashley's head, Ashley was screaming at Dexter for doing so, Little Tim was boxing Nosebleed, and Madeline was dancing topless, trying to get their attention. Charlie had his arms around a girl with pink hair. He saw me see him and let her go. He shouted something across the room at me I couldn't hear. I felt dizzy and needed a beer. I hopped back into the hallway and into the kitchen. Some guy leaned into the open fridge. I patted him on the shoulder.

"Can I get one?" I asked.

"What do you want?"

"Whatever."

He stood up and handed me a PBR. His body was sinewy and his face was spectacular. There was something glamorous about him. Mysterious. Imagine if Keanu Reeves spent a week sleeping on the street. An old I HEART NY shirt hung on his broad shoulders and his jeans were held up with a spiked belt. Worn-out skate shoes hinted he knew some tricks. His smile was big and crooked, his nose was broad, and his eyes were glittering. His eyelashes and eyebrows were dark and thick. The hair on his head was dyed half-black, half-orange.

"I'm Jake," he said.

"I'm Kat." My stomach hurt.

Charlie walked up behind him. "Jake, you met Kit Kat?"

"A second ago," he breathed, maintaining eye contact with me.

"You guys are friends?" I asked Charlie.

"Jake lives in Pittsboro. He never hangs out," Charlie stated.

"I'm moving here, actually." Jake smirked.

"Really? Since when?" barked Charlie.

"Since now." Jake smiled at me.

"A'right, I'll be over there," Charlie said, and walked away.

"Listen." Jake had a soft, raspy voice.

"Yeah?" I leaned toward him. He smelled like coffee.

"I gotta bounce."

"Oh," I said, disappointed.

"I know we just met . . ."

"Yeah?"

"Can I have your number?"

I grabbed a piece of paper from the trash on the counter and a pen from my purse and wrote it down with my name. He took the paper and said, "I like how you wrote that without the dashes between the numbers."

I shrugged. "Dashes are a waste of space."

When Jake left I chugged my beer between two giant skinheads. Then I grabbed another can and looked for Charlie. Everyone was messed up. The kids who did downers lay on the floor, in the bathtub, on the couches. The ones who did uppers were fighting and screwing. The whole place was trashed. Well, more trashed than usual.

I found Charlie back in the Party Room, hitting a bong. He looked up at me with red eyes and went, "I knew that would happen." I said, "What?" He was like, "Never mind." I sat down next to him and he put his arm around me. He was like, "You want a hit of this?" I didn't but I said that I did. Dexter punched a hole in the wall, Ashley spit beer on Nosebleed, and Madeline made out with Little Tim.

CHAPEL HILL COMICS

The first hangover of my life was out of this world. I'd heard people talk about hangovers. They sounded annoying but doable. Something you grit your teeth at and get over. Maybe what I had wasn't a hangover. It couldn't be; this couldn't be what other people feel, then choose to continue living. To continue drinking. What did I do wrong? I had been drunk plenty of times without feeling this way. God finally found out and decided to punish me. *Thou shalt not mix PBR and whiskey.* It was like that book, *War and Peace*, which I never finished. Hangovers represent justice. The suffering to pay for your sins. When the hangover is over, you must not feel guilt, for you served your punishment. But this hangover felt eternal. Each breath I took was a cursed miracle. Each step, baffling. My survival was a mystery to science. My dad saw me in the kitchen that morning and laughed. "Oh, buddy, you look like me." He handed me a gallon of water. "Next time," he advised, "drink this *before* going to bed." I said there won't be a next time. He said, laughing, "Yeah, right," and disappeared into the garage. I lugged the gallon to the bus stop and chugged it all on the ride. Then I peed myself a little bit on the way to the bookstore.

My brain buzzed so loud I couldn't think. Flipping through magazines was painful. Images blurred into barf and words dashed around like flies. It made me nauseous. I groaned and tossed *Vice* magazine onto the chair across mine. It hit the empty gallon bottle. She stared at me. "What do *you* want?" I asked her. She didn't respond. I needed backup. I stuck a BE RIGHT BACK sign on the front door, got a supersized Diet Coke from McDonald's, and headed over to Chapel Hill Comics. Bob said "Whoa" when I walked in. "What?" I groaned. Today would *not* be the day I lose my virginity to him.

"You look rough," he said.

"What do you mean?" I croaked.

"What are you wearing?"

I didn't have time to change that morning or I would have missed the bus. The raggy dress hung on by a thread. My hair was a mess and I stank of smoke. If I took my dark Ray-Bans off I'd shrivel up like a vampire. "I thought I looked cool."

"Well, keep thinking."

"Shut up. You got my Clowes?"

"Oh, right." Bob shuffled around under the counter.

He held it up like a prize. *Like a Velvet Glove Cast in Iron*. I'd been waiting on this for weeks. I could tell it was a masterpiece.

"Thanks, dude." I grabbed the comic and rummaged through my purse. "How much is it?"

"This one's on me."

"Are you serious?"

"Yeah, but you've gotta make it up to me."

"Really?" Gulp. "How?"

"Listen to my radio show tonight."

"Duh, I always do."

"Good girl." Bob changed the Radiohead song that was playing.

"Why'd you skip that? I love Radiohead."

"Ugh, you would." Bob rolled his eyes and disappeared into the stock room. I headed back to work with my life-saving comic and soda.

Mom picked me up from the bookstore and drove me to my piano lesson. She asked how work was and I said okay. She asked how school's going and I said fine. She asked how piano is and I said good. Mom and I were really close when I was little. Best friends until a couple of years ago. I began to hide things from her. To avoid pissing her off. When she was mad she didn't yell or punish me. But her passivity made me feel like a little shit.

Mom was beautiful. She had classic Slavic features and never wore makeup. The only thing she put on her face was L'Oréal moisturizer that smelled like roses. On special occasions, like when she got her PhD, she wore a trace of pink Chanel lipstick. She kept the same tube for years. She only wore jeans, Converse, and T-shirts. She looked like a teenager. Her favorite store was the Gap. She had a naturally good figure and never seemed to fuss about it. Dad was cute, too. They met as kids and were the ultimate hot commie couple. They'd ride the Mediterranean coast on Dad's bike and get high. Dad played guitar and had tons of curly blond hair. Mom said that's what drew her to him.

By thirty he was bald. "Never fall for a boy's hair," she warned me. My parents loved each other, still. They even *liked* each other. I'd catch them kissing and go, "Ew." Dad would reply, "You prefer I hit her?"

Mom hoped I'd go to college. She was obsessed with the idea. Mom loved school and she thought everyone else should. If she could, she'd be in school forever. That's what academia is all about. I hated regular, mandatory school so much, I couldn't fathom choosing further education . . . and paying for it. I barely talked her into letting me audition for the arts academy. Boarding school for musicians. Heaven. The idea was I'd spend junior and senior year there. I'd graduate from there. Of course she was sad at the idea of me moving away so soon. But she approved of my ambition and the idea of me getting "away from bad friends." She told me it made her sad to see whom I hung out with. So I avoided letting her do so.

One night, after the Adderall Incident, Mom dropped me off at Cat's Cradle, and Jeremy, the boy who arranged for me to get the pills from this other kid, yelled at her from across the parking lot. He was like, "Kat's mom. It wasn't me. I wasn't the one who sold her the drugs." After I got suspended, I wasn't allowed to hang out with him anymore. He didn't realize what he did only made it worse. Everyone in the parking lot looked at Mom and she got upset. I felt so guilty when she drove away.

"How could he yell at me?" she wondered for days. In the Old Country kids respect each other's parents, or something.

Mom shouldn't have had me. If she were free she could focus on her research and have fun with Dad. She was always doing math equations or studying or stressing about something. Mom supported me. She got me the *No Thanks! The '70s Punk Rebellion* box set for my sixteenth birthday. She bought me the first Strokes album as a surprise. And Radiohead's *Kid A* album. She took me to see Sonic Youth in concert when I was fourteen. She was cool. She just wished my interests didn't attract *those* types of people. The bad kids. *Mom, I'm the bad kid.*

My piano teacher got mean when I was sloppy. His disapproval killed me because I was obsessed with him. He was in his thirties, and he dressed badly and had a wife. He was a genius piano player, like a prodigy. I couldn't imagine why he was stuck teaching dickheads in Durham. He ate an average of six Altoids throughout our lessons.

"What's the left hand doing?" He sucked his mint.

I fumbled through the *Minute Waltz*. "Playing?"

"Everything but playing."

"Sorry." My hands were shaking all day.

"Start again. And take those damn rings off."

I slid the rings off my fingers and set them on top of the piano. He picked them up and put them in his pocket. Yeah, I was in love. It didn't make sense. I either liked wild boys or hopeless dorks. Could he tell I was hungover?

"Enough of this." He closed my Chopin book and sat next to me on the bench. He usually sat in his own chair. Feeling his thighs next to mine meant I was in trouble.

"Let's improvise."

I failed at jazz even on a good day. “Can we do Bill Evans? ‘Someday My Prince Will Come’?”

“No.” I could smell the mint on his breath. “You already know that one.”

He pulled out *The Real Book* and flipped to some madness from Miles Davis. I didn’t stand a chance. I cringed through my chords and improvisations. It was mortifying, feeling his disappointment.

“When’s your audition?” he asked as I packed up.

“In April.”

He whistled. “You better get serious.”

I still needed a recommendation letter from him. I’d ask next lesson.

“I’ll kill it next week, I promise.” I didn’t believe a word I said.

I got home and showered forever. I felt grime and sludge slide off me. I trimmed my hair. Bangs are easy to cut because they’re right there. The rest is tricky. I sat on the sink and used a hand mirror to check on the back as I chopped away at it. My hair was always uneven but nobody noticed when I wore it up. When the hairs from the sink were successfully transferred into the toilet, I changed into pajamas.

In the kitchen I made grilled cheese. My parents were eating spaghetti and watching TV. “Good night,” I grumbled, climbing up the stairs with my sandwich. I turned my radio to 89.3, the student radio station. I lay on my floor and ate my dinner while plucking my eyebrows under the light of a desk lamp. I did this for an hour each night. Nothing beat the cheap, criminal thrill of overplucking them. It was personal vandalism.

Bob's voice came on. It was made for the radio. Low and soothing. He talked about the songs he played, then said, "This next track is dedicated to the best set of pigtails in Chapel Hill."

My heart beat in my head. The song was French techno. A deliberately sexy song.

I thought about him thinking about me as I put my hand down my pants. "*Kat*," Mom yelled from downstairs.

"*What*." I froze. "You've got a phone call."

Damn it. I took my hand out of my pants and sat up.

"*Bring the phone*," I screamed.

Mom knocked on my door and I got up and she handed me the receiver. I slammed the door behind her.

"Hello?"

"Kit Kat."

"Charlie?" He never called me.

"Do you wanna go out with me?"

"Where?"

"I mean, be my girlfriend."

"Oh. Really?"

"Yeah."

"Okay."

"Cool. See you at school."

He hung up. My song was over.

WEAVER STREET MARKET

I hated Sundays. The day of dread. I spent the whole day fearing the next. I couldn't enjoy the time off because I was too busy watching the clock. Sundays represent humanity, the pain of existing, knowing it's all gonna end tragically. I couldn't stand the existential panic. Or maybe I just hated school.

Only the mornings were bearable because of breakfast. Mom drove us to Weaver Street Market, a co-op hippie grocery and café. We'd been going there since I was a kid. When we lived in Carrboro we could walk here. Mom liked taking walks when she was stressed and back then she was always stressed. I remember holding her hand on Pine Street. I wore a blue suede coat with round buttons and flower clips in my hair. She'd get me a fruit tart and hot chocolate. It was a big deal, we didn't tell Dad we spent money like that. The café used to be tiny and the dining area had mosquito repellent lamps hanging from the ceiling. Coffins for bugs. They transformed it into something sleek and tasteless. The bugs were replaced by "liberals" who care about money, Jesus, and basketball.

Mom read the newspaper across from me. She loved reading more than anything. She'd read the back of a cereal box, the label on a shampoo bottle, and graffiti on a wall before talking—her last resort. I learned to bring comic books when we hung out. I read *Like a Velvet Glove Cast in Iron* and managed to eat half a pancake. They didn't make grilled cheese at Weaver Street.

Anything after breakfast was tragic. We were glum. Sunday was Dad's only day out of his work garage, and he spent it in our garage. Mom studied and made me study. I couldn't wait for it to be over and I was sad that it would be.

That Sunday was worse than the other Sundays because that Sunday I was worried about my first Monday as Charlie's girlfriend. What would he want from me? I didn't know how to do anything. What would I wear? On the floor I decided on a classic: the oversized jeans with the deadly safety pin, my Casualties T-shirt, and boots. Or . . . *or, or, or* . . . I fell asleep on the pile of clothes.

I woke up too early, at six. Downstairs I quietly made coffee. Dad was walking the dog. I watched music videos on VH1 until Mom woke up. Then I showered in her bathroom. In her mirror I looked faint. Pale. Sick. Would he want me to have sex with him *immediately*? Where? On the hill? In front of our friends?

I panicked at the bus stop, I freaked on the bus, and I hyperventilated in homeroom. No Charlie yet. I had a Nokia flip phone but he didn't so he couldn't even text me. I saw Ashley and waved. "Cool party," I said.

She scoffed. "Have you seen Charlie?"

"I was just gonna ask you that."

She smirked at me. "So you don't know where your own boyfriend is?" I didn't know what to say.

"Off to a great start." She laughed, walking off.

The periods passed and I sat on the hill at lunch. Charlie finally showed up. He was holding a large blue Care Bear. He handed it to me.

"For Kit Kat."

I took the bear and hugged it. It was bigger than my torso. "Wow, thanks, Charlie. I love the Care Bears."

"I know."

"Where have you been all day?"

"Stealing money to get you this."

I laughed. "No, for real?"

He sat down next to me and lit a cigarette. "For real."

Ashley and Nosebleed showed up. Everyone talked shit as usual. Charlie walked me to precalc. "What are you doing tonight?" he asked.

"I can't go out on school nights. Unless there's a show."

"That sucks."

"I know."

"Let's ditch class?"

"I have tests today."

"Bummer."

"Yeah . . . but. This weekend is Trippy Dope."

"Yeah and?"

"Wanna go with me?"

"Okay."

"I already have my ticket."

"Cool."

He kissed me and walked outside and off campus.

The next day was the same. And the day after that. And the entire school week. Charlie walked me to classes and gave me kisses in the hallway. After school he would hang out at Dexter's while I stayed home, studying and playing piano. He never called me and I never called him. We didn't email or text each other. On the hill at lunch he'd hug me and call me his girlfriend in front of everyone, but it felt forced. I worried through all of my classes.

Do they all know we haven't gone on a real date yet? Do they know we never even French kissed? Is this a practical joke? Are they all laughing at me?

I was nervous all the time. My confusion and anxiety blocked any potential passion or intimacy. *He's treating me like a child. Because I am one. Poor Charlie. What did he get himself into? He's sick of me. Looking for a way out. He'll dump me soon. I'll have to make up for it this weekend . . . OR ELSE. Trippy Dope is playing Saturday. Perfect. I'll stay in Friday night to save my best outfit . . . I can't meet up with Bob Saturday. I'll have to see Trippy Dope as a virgin.*

CARRBURRITOS

Whenever a band came through, they ate at Carrburritos. They did so because (1) it was across the street from Cat's Cradle and (2) it was the best Mexican food in town and probably the world, including Mexico. Carrburritos was jammed between a meditation studio and a tattoo shop. The space was cozy. Square tables were sealed in bright plastic. Steel chairs had cushy foam seats. Amateur still life hung on the walls.

You walked in and grabbed a tray. Then you got a drink from the fridge. You waited in line until it was your turn to tell the "chefs" your order. There was an assembly-line kitchen so you'd watch your food get made. Everyone who worked at Carrburritos was hip and hot. Boys with backwards hats, sweaty black shirts, and bad attitudes. I always got nervous when it was my turn to order. Carrburritos didn't have grilled cheese sandwiches but they did have cheese quesadillas. Fried flour chips were their specialty.

All salsas were made in-house, super spicy. The margaritas were sick but I wasn't allowed to order them. Charlie got me one.

Whoever played at Cat's Cradle said something about Carrburritos onstage.

Every band was like, "We hate this shithole state but Carrburritos made it great." And I could say "every band" because I've seen a thousand shows at Cat's Cradle. Everyone came through from Iggy Pop to the Yeah Yeah Yeahs. The Dirty South sucks but my town had some perks.

We all went to Carrburritos before Cat's Cradle because there was a chance to run into the bands. A flock of punks would split a burrito and order of chips because they were too broke, too high, or too excited to eat. Everyone wanted to be a groupie, even the boys. The boys called sluts "groupies" and groupies "sluts" because they were jealous.

They thought girls had it easy. They thought we used boys because we were too lazy to do stuff on our own. They had it twisted.

"Girls bang rock stars because they want to *be* rock stars," I explained.

"Girls can be rock stars." Nosebleed chewed with his mouth open.

"Yeah, sure, Debbie Harry and Patti Smith. The Runaways and Bikini Kill. The problem is—"

"The problem is girls suck." Little Tim cackled.

"For a *million* reasons, it's harder for a woman to be a rock star. And when she is one, she doesn't get to be a rock star in the *same way*. If you say otherwise, you're a dickhead."

"I never said I wasn't a dickhead," Little Tim joked.

"Look what happened to Courtney Love." I knew I lost my audience but couldn't help pushing on. "It's not just rock and roll, it's real life. Girls date bad boys because they want to be bad, because they aren't allowed to be bad on their own. When they *are* bad on their own they get punished. Do you get it?"

"Kat, chill. I just called that wannabe groupie a skank because . . . well, look at her." Dexter pointed to the heavily made up girl across the dining room. Everyone giggled in agreement.

Skank.

I sipped my margarita. I usually avoided talking but I couldn't when I cared about something. Of course Dexter didn't "get it." Ashley was cooler than him but she was still known as "Dexter's girlfriend."

The tequila tickled the back of my neck, then pressed on my shoulders. Relaxing syrup drizzled all over me. I sat back and chilled, as instructed. Charlie took my hand under the table. I couldn't believe these were my friends. I was having one of those moments, when I felt "in," for real. I thought, *I am the girl in the movie. I am the protagonist.* Then Ashley came back from the bathroom and I snapped out of it. Maybe I could be the supporting actress.

CAT'S CRADLE

Before the show we drank Mad Dog in the Cradle parking lot. It was hard to get booze from the bar since they checked IDs. Charlie and Dexter usually managed but relying on them was a drag. Ashley and I chugged as much as we could. Mad Dog tasted like gummy bears, if you let gummy bears sit in the glove compartment of a car on a hot summer day.

We finished the bottle and piled into the club. It was packed and smoky. None of us cared for the opening band. We stopped by the merch table. A shirt was twenty-five dollars, hoodies thirty-five. Crazy. Charlie told me he wanted to go outside to the smoking area. We were just outside, I said. He went outside anyway. Everyone followed him but me.

I dove into the crowd and let the energy conquer me. Nothing felt like a mosh pit.

I never pushed but I let myself be pushed. I always ended up battered and bruised but nothing serious. Blue spots to show off at school. I crowd surfed once. It was thrilling. Sometimes jerks ruined it—like *now*. This wasn't moshing, this was violence. It was too late for me to get out, I was right in the middle of it.

"Dude, no punching," I yelled. Cartoons see stars when they get beat up. That was me, I was the Wile E. Coyote after falling off a cliff, or Daffy Duck with his head blasted off by a rifle. All I saw was black and polka dots. "Fucking skinheads." I got hit in the back of the head and body-slammed into the front of the stage. Ribs smashed. I couldn't breathe. I pulled myself to the side of the stage while people crashed into me. I found a corner next to a door and collapsed. A few songs passed.

"Hey, kid. You can't sit there."

"I'm resting," I answered the floor, my head between my knees.

"Rest somewhere else."

I looked up at a roadie. You can tell a roadie is a roadie. They've got beer bellies from backstage booze, bad posture from sleeping on buses, dirty clothes from sweaty grunt work, and a face that says *I wanna be a musician but don't have the talent*. "I'm hurt. Give me a minute."

"I don't got a minute."

I gazed at the furious crowd. "Where am I supposed to go? Those dudes beat the crap outta me."

"Goddammit, kid."

I groaned helplessly.

"Okay. Come with me."

The roadie pulled me up by the pits and dragged me backstage. I leaned on him, relieved. Then I realized: *backstage* . . .

leads to outside. Dammit, Kat. You fell for it. Trusting a roadie? He'll kick you to the curb, if you're lucky. More likely he'll rape and kill you before throwing your body in the dumpster. I closed my eyes, expecting the worst. I opened them in heaven.

Years of my life have been committed to fantasizing about the backstage of Cat's Cradle. Several versions of it lived inside my head. One was mirrors, tinfoil, and cement, like Andy Warhol's Factory. The other was velvet and disco balls, like Studio 54. The CBGB's-inspired version involved flyers, graffiti, blood, and piss. This was neither. The real-life backstage, the one I found myself in, by some miracle, was dull. But glorious with austerity.

The lighting was unflattering, the furniture was unremarkable, and the coffee table was crowded with junk food. No opium, supermodels, or glamour in sight. But I didn't need that. I had Trippy Dope.

He sat on the sofa smoking a cigarette. Two, actually. One hung from his mouth while he ashed another in a soda can. He was wearing only leather pants. A large lump lurked under his pocket. Dirty hair fell down his back. Puffy bags hung around his eyes. Hollow cheeks made his face feline and vicious. He smelled like a farm animal and trembled like a stray. God himself.

"Yo Trip, can this kid sit? She's hurt, blocking the door, I gotta set up."

"She's hurt?" He winked at me. "Never heard that before."

I was stunned by him and still in shock from earlier. Mute.

"She's fine," he said to the roadie. "Sit down, kid," he said at me, patting the space next to him. I sat where his hand was.

The roadie left and suddenly I was a l o n e

in a room

WITH **TRIPPY DOPE** . . .

If my friends could see me. They'd be so proud. I can't wait to tell them. They'll be so jealous. They'll wanna die. They'll wanna kill me. They won't believe it. They'll never believe it . . . they'll think I'm lying. They'll say I'm a poseur. They'll totally hate me. I can't tell them. No, never. It's a secret. I'm not here. I should go—

"So you a groupie?" Trippy offered a smoke.

"I'm a fan." I took the cigarette.

"A fan of what?"

"Are you kidding?" I gawked and the cigarette fell out of my mouth. "I'm your *biggest fan.*" I picked it up and let him light it.

"You're 'into the music'?" he said, quoting the air.

"Of course." He seemed bored. I was saying something wrong, or leaving something out. I panicked. Of course, I forgot to talk about him. "But you aren't just an artist, you're a . . . phenomenon, a provocateur . . ."

"Do I provoke you?" He got up, stumbled around, and grabbed a bottle of whiskey. I didn't answer. He collapsed next to me and poked me in the ribs.

"Ow." I grimaced. "I got slammed in the pit." I reminded him.

He ignored it and kept his finger planted in a soft spot between my bones. "Who brought you here?"

"The roadie?" I gulped.

"Why are you here?" He released the finger and leered.

A part of me was always here, I thought. I didn't say it out loud, thank God.

"Is this a game for you?" He chugged from the bottle and passed it to me. I took a swig, held the liquor in my mouth, and wondered. What was I doing wrong? This was my dream come true, and it didn't feel good. Trippy wasn't being mean to me, but he wasn't being nice, either. He didn't like me. I wanted to be on his good side but a concrete wall stood in my way, trapping me on his bad side. I gulped the booze and it burned my throat.

"You're on in five." The roadie barged in.

"All right, kid, later." Trippy pushed himself to his feet.

"Wait. I'm coming," I pleaded.

"I thought you were hurt?"

"I wanna watch." But I hugged my ribs at the thought of it.

"You're pitiful. Don't move."

He slammed the door behind him.

I flipped open my phone.

Nosebleed: "Trip is coming."

Little Tim: "Where R U"

Unknown: "ITS C-ROCK FRONT STAGE"

"I'm backstage," I typed, then deleted before sending.

I closed my phone and closed my eyes and listened to the show.

I'll tell Nosebleed I was there the whole time, in the mosh pit, too busy punching skinheads to check my phone. I'll tell Charlie I got wasted and spent the whole set puking in the toilets. I'll tell Dexter I scored drugs and overdosed in the parking lot. I'll tell Little Tim I walked out for a smoke and couldn't get back in. I'll tell Ashley I hopped a train and ended up in Mississippi and found Josh and lived happily ever after. I'll tell them to forget me because I died.

Ten tracks passed before I heard the door open. A light body plopped down next to me. The body smelled like candy. Not Trippy. I opened my eyes.

"Don't mind me, keep sleeping."

"I'm not sleeping." I looked her over in awe. She had a lime-green buzz cut and a rose tattoo on her neck. She was wearing red shorts, red boots, and a red leather jacket.

Her tights were pink. "Are you Trippy's girlfriend?" I asked.

"No. I'm a writer."

"Cool. I'm Kat."

"Sabrina."

She picked through the stuff on the table, trying to find a drink.

"All of those cans have ash in them," I said expertly.

"I figured." She took a potato chip out of a bag and held it in her hand.

"So what do you write?"

"I'm the editor of *Gunshot* magazine."

"Is it like *Vice*?"

"We're more hard-core. And online only." She smelled the potato chip and carefully placed it back on the table.

"So it's a weblog?"

"A *blog* is a *hobby* for housewives, conspiracy theorists, and virgins." It sounded like something she'd rehearsed, or said so many times before that it became an automatic reply. "I've got an office in Brooklyn and millions of readers . . . I don't know why I'm explaining myself to you?" She was worked up.

"I didn't mean it that way. I don't know anything."

She brushed it off. "Online publishing is the future."

"I love magazines but I hate carrying them around."

"You're funny, Kat. Mind if I record us?"

She put a black tape recorder on the table, between the ashtray and beer. "What are you doing back here?"

"I just got slammed in the mosh pit and this roadie let me chill backstage. I got to meet Trippy Dope. Have you met him?"

"Oh, honey. I've been on the road with him for weeks. I'm writing his tour diary."

"That's amazing. Are you having the best time?"

"It's good material."

"I'm so jealous."

She grinned. "So you a groupie or what?"

"I'm just a fan."

"But you're hot for him?"

"Duh, I mean, he's the coolest."

"How old are you?"

"Sixteen."

"That's legal here? You know he's twenty-seven?"

"No way." I didn't know how old I thought he was. I'd never considered it. But twenty-seven seemed ancient.

The crowd went wild. "The show must be over," she said.

Fans chanted for an encore as Trippy came back to us. He smiled big. He was bleeding all over. The sight of him thrilled me again.

"No encore tonight?" Sabrina asked.

"Nah, fuck these hicks." Trippy drained the rest of the whiskey.

"How was it?" I probed, beaming. I thought of asking if he saw my friends. *Did they have fun? Did they miss me?*

"Nothing special." He threw himself on the couch.

Sabrina took a few pictures of him and he posed. She messed up his hair and smeared the blood on his face. She said, "Put Kat in your lap." And he did. She took pictures of us. He hugged my waist and I couldn't help but smile.

"Y'all look incredible. I'm gonna piss, don't move." She grabbed her camera and tape recorder and left us alone. I felt his bulge on my butt. Trippy breathed into my hair and went, "You mind if I don't fuck you?"

"What?" I stiffened.

"I'm wasted. You can tell your friends we did it."

I slid off his lap. "Can I have a smoke?"

He handed me his pack. "You don't fool me."

"What do you mean?" I lit myself one.

"Are you for real?"

"In what way?"

"You wanna be in this world, you gotta be hard-core."

"I am hard-core."

He laughed. "I don't mean moshing. That's for boys."

"Where's the after-party?" Sabrina burst in with high spirits. White powder clumped inside her left nostril.

"Kat should know." Trippy threw me a testing look.

"Dexter's Lab. I can ask my friends?"

"What's that? A club?"

"It's a house, down the street, they've got this amazing room, with a fridge for a door, and—"

"I'm not going to a redneck meth lab," Trippy teased.

"We don't do meth. Dexter did it *once* as a joke."

"Sab, back to the suite."

"Nice meeting you, Kat." They left faster than I could say *fuckup*. I sat in silent remorse till the roadie showed up with a death stare. *Fuckin' roadies. At least he didn't dumpster your body*. I slipped out. The air outside was fresh and free. The collective relief of an exhausting show. My ribs hurt and so did my feelings. I couldn't tell why, exactly. Because I missed the show? My crew was nowhere in sight.

Mom was waiting in the Honda.

* * *

GUNSHOT MAGAZINE

TRIPPY DOPE DIARY, PART 13: CAT'S CRADLE, NC

By Sabrina Mink

Sunday, January 18, 2004, 9:02 a.m.

*I'm out of clean clothes, out of my mind, and out of things to say about Trippy Dope. Please indulge and allow me to fluff this puff piece by stuffing it with grease. We drove all night and through dawn to make it from Memphis to Chapel Hill. We were put up in the Siena Hotel, a real treat. I haven't seen a proper suite in ages. Think: luxurious relaxation for old racists. They had a gorgeous breakfast in the banquet hall but it was expen$ive as f*ck. The bellhop gave me the 411: right up the street we could cop the dankest biscuits in town. (Never ignore a bellhop's tip, especially when he's cute.) Sunrise Biscuit Kitchen didn't disappoint. I got a loaded egg, bacon, and cheese. Trippy got a plain biscuit because he's a b*tch. Sunrise doesn't have good coffee so they suggested we go up the street, to Caffé Driade.*

*This sh*t was legit. European style. They take their time pressing espressos. The barista was a hottie, too. I asked if he was going to Trippy's show and he said, "F*ck that guy." Then Trippy came out of the bathroom and ordered his latte . . . the look on the barista's face. I gave the poor kid a fat tip.*

We took caffeinated catnaps in our suite and primped one last time . . . as I said, we're out of clean clothes, so Trippy wore leather pants with no shirt, shoes, or underwear. I was chic, as usual. (Heard of hand-washing in a tub and drying with a hair dryer?)

Before sound check we fed at Carrburritos. It's a cheap Mexican spot with a heart of gold. Sex on a plate. The flour chips were a bizarre touch. I know what you're thinking: "Since when is Gunshot a food magazine?" Sorry . . . food is what the South's famous for. (Okay, the South is famous for worse things but this definitely isn't a political magazine.) Moving on . . .

Cat's Cradle is iconic. Everyone who matters has come through here. Legends, living and dead. I could list them all but you know what? Google it. I'm convinced Cat's Cradle is the only institution keeping this town running. Well, Cat's is actually in Carrboro, Chapel Hill's hippie sister. The two blend into each other, you only notice the difference once it's too late . . . hah. The show was absurd, disastrous, and epic, as always. We got a few injured soldiers, casualties of the mosh pit. They sacrificed themselves for their god.

One tiny sex martyr (pictured below) made quite the impression on our leading man. She used being "wounded in the pit" as an excuse to "recover" backstage . . . is that what the kids call getting busy? Girlies, take note: These days it takes a special edge to get what you want. Especially if what you want . . . is Trippy Dope.

*(Pictured: Trippy Dope postshow with Kat,
local teenage groupie)*

It's been a hell of a ride but I can't wait to get the hell off this tour bus and back into civilization. Oh, and the gym . . . I'll need at least six hours to work off that biscuit.

STAY SCANDALOUS
Sabrina

* * *

MY ROOM

I stared at my wall for hours. Pictures from my disposable camera taped everywhere. Notes from Lucy, birthday cards from boys. Band posters. I glared at the Ramones and begged them for answers. They stared back blankly. I moved my eyes over to the Strokes. Strung-out beauties standing against a wall. "What should I do?" I asked. Julian Casablancas answered, "Roll with it." Next to my record player sat the giant blue Care Bear. He made me feel guilty. I resented him for it. My phone rang. I opened and closed it to hang up. I left the texts unanswered.

Nosebleed: "U fucked Trippy?"

Little Tim: "Nasty bitch."

Unknown: "CALL C-ROCK @ DEXTER'S"

I hid my phone under my pillow and opened my laptop, *again*. The more I looked at it the crazier I felt. Surreal. I only checked *Gunshot* that morning because Sabrina told me about it. As the homepage loaded, I thought I must be seeing things, still drunk from the night before. But nope, there it was: my dumb face next to Trippy Dope's. There were his famous hands, around my waist. There were my scrawny legs, crossed with his. Our faces looked high and horny. My eyes were glazed and my grin sly. Trippy a sex-crazed devil on my shoulder. Sabrina captured an innocent moment cleverly. Artfully. Trickery. My brush with glory mortified me. Being seen with my idol was a dream come true. But not like this. *Not like this*. I had nothing against groupies, in theory. They had their reasons, their history . . . I did have something against being falsely exposed as a groupie.

I'd worked hard to establish myself as *one of the crew*. Girls who slept with rock stars weren't taken seriously. I wanted my own legacy. Too bad, so sad. There was nothing I could do now. Press was truth. It even convinced me, as I read it and reread it: "Kat, local teenage groupie."

KAT.

KAT KAT KAT*katkatkatkatkatkatkatkatkatkatkatk*

LOCAAAAL tEEN*AGE(....)*

(teenteenteen)

!GrOUpIE!

At first I thought, *Nobody reads this crap, I only checked because she practically begged me to*. But then I opened my MSN inbox . . . kids I hadn't talked to since sixth grade emailed me about it. My AIM chat was bonkers. Like a winning Vegas slot machine. I couldn't stomach answering anyone. The critics had mixed, positive reviews of my behavior . . . but I couldn't relish the attention. *It isn't true.* I set my away message to: "I don't give a damn 'bout my reputation / You're living in the past it's a new generation / A girl can do what she wants to do and that's / What I'm gonna do."

I was toast.

Mmm, toast. I snuck downstairs and made a grilled cheese. My parents were off somewhere, with the dog. I woke up too late for Weaver Street. Back in my room I plucked my eyebrows for an hour, rearranged my closet, cut a shirt so badly I had to throw it away. I sifted through old *Archie* comics but found no relief in Jughead. I became so desperate I cracked open my chemistry book. Then I slammed it shut. Not that desperate. To play piano I'd have to go back downstairs and that was too much work.

I sight-read Beethoven under my covers. My piano teacher said it's better than nothing. He told me that back in the old days, whenever those were, composers and musicians would sight-read sheet music on a long train ride. After a dozen hours or so they'd be able to sit down at their instrument and play the song they read perfectly upon arriving at their destination.

It sounded like bullshit to me. But now nothing seemed like *not*-bullshit. Still . . . I longed to be in the past, on a carriage, headed to some stuffy recital . . . before the world wide web showed up and complicated our lives. Before I was me and Trippy was Trippy and the Cat's Cradle was the center of the universe.

I got another text. This one from Ashley. She never texted me. I only had her number saved for Charlie's sake, in case he needed to call her while with me. I groaned, flipping the phone open and expecting the worst.

"KAT UR A FUCKIN LEGEND."

KAT

UR

A FUCKIN

L E G E N D.

Legend.

Le ge nd .

Leg
END. *Lege* nd. .

L *egend* .

Mom came into my room without knocking.

L e g e n d .

She was like, "Are you going to study?"
Legend. "Yes."
"Need anything from the store?"

Legend. "No."

"Wanna come with me?"

Legend. "Too tired."

She left me alone with my thoughts.

Legend

Legend

Legend.

I didn't reply because that would ruin it. Out my window I watched the deer in our yard. Dad left carrots for them every night. There was a mom deer and two baby deer. They weren't babies anymore. One of them was growing his horns out. Poor thing.

Childhood is over, buddy.

Ashley texted me again. "Meet @ Timberlyne? Free popcorn."

TIMBERLYNE CINEMAS

Ashley had a paying job. Maybe that's how she got her clothes. She didn't dress cool at work. They made her wear an ugly mauve uniform. Of course she beat the laws of physics and fashion and looked good in it. She worked the concession at Timberlyne. Free popcorn and movies for her friends. This was the first time she invited me.

Mom thought she was dropping me off to meet Lucy. She was like, "I miss her. Can I say hi?"

I had to lie. "She's already inside, I'm late for the flick." I hated lying but I was getting better at it: keep it simple. The more lies you pile on the more you'll have to remember. I walked inside and saw Ashley behind the counter. Fear struck my heart as it always did when I saw her. She waved at me eagerly.

"Oh my God, bitch. I hate you!" she shrieked.

"That makes two of us."

"So? How was he?" She was thirsting for info. Her eye contact made me squirm. She never spoke to me directly. Her presence in my life thus far only served to make me invisible. Now I was in her spotlight. And it burned. I played along because I didn't know what else to do. *How was he?*

"Who, Trippy?"

"No, Santa."

"Hah, right." I cleared my throat and felt flushed. "He was . . . amazing?"

"I want details."

A customer saved me by asking Ashley for Twizzlers. As she rang him up, rolling her eyes, I considered telling the truth. That would be foolish. Why kill such a surreal moment? *Just roll with it*, as Julian Casablancas advised.

"I thought you were a prude," she continued. "No offense."

"None taken."

"I didn't know you had it in you."

"Same."

"We should hang out."

"Yeah." Weren't we hanging out now?

"Come to the mall with me next weekend."

"Really? I mean, sure."

"Do you lift?"

"Shoplift? Yeah, CDs, sometimes."

"Oh, babe. I'll show you how it's done."

"Cool." Shoplifting CDs was really hard, actually. Taking off the crazy plastic wrapping under your clothes so the alarm won't go off? Those plastic covers were hard to take off even with the full privacy of a bedroom, with scissors. I had a special technique, using my nails, which took months to perfect. Anyway, I was grateful she wanted to show me anything.

"So what do you wanna watch?"

"Oh . . . nothing?" Did she think I came to see a movie? Was it stupid that I came just to talk to her?

"You can't hang around. My manager will kill me. Pick any show." She handed me a popcorn and Coke. I shuffled off and slipped inside the nearest dark room. I didn't pause to read the screens because I felt like she was watching me from behind and it made me nervous.

I picked the wrong room. It was showing a horror movie. I couldn't stand horror. Lucy loved scary movies and made us watch them every Friday. Her house, her rules. I'd get so scared I could never fall asleep. She'd be out like a light and I'd watch her ceiling till dawn. My parents would pick me up on Saturday looking like a zombie.

I tried to shut my eyes through the screening but the sounds were too gruesome.

Through my hands the emergency exit glowed. This was an emergency, for me.

"Had to dip. See u 2mrw." I texted Ashley from the bus stop. I'd tell Mom that. Lucy drove me home.

Ashley will think you're such a loser for leaving. You blew the one shot at being her friend. Why'd you pick that theater? Why are you such a pussy? You're the only bitch who can't sit through a horror flick. Oh, well, life sucks. Ashley texted when I was on the bus.

"Sux you left. Can't w8 2 c u @ skool."

"Is this a joke? What the fuck is happening?" I said out loud.

"Watch your mouth, miss," the bus driver advised.

"Sorry, ma'am." I reread her text all the way home.

THE HILL

I've been a bad, bad girl. I've been careless with a delicate man. Charlie didn't come to school all week. I hadn't heard from him but I could guess it was over between us. I didn't blame him. According to everyone I cheated on him with a rock star.

"Y'all heard from C-Rock?" I asked the hill crew.

"Partying." Nosebleed shrugged.

"At Dexter's?"

"I guess." Classic Nosebleed.

"He's in Durham," Ashley said.

"What's he doing there?"

"Screwing his new girlfriend." Madeline snickered.

Nobody asked you, bitch. "New girlfriend?" I gasped.

"The poor guy had to rebound," Ashley explained.

"Yeah . . . but what about school?"

"What about it?" They all laughed.

Charlie's absence was a relief. He'd be pissed that I "cheated" on him, even though I didn't, really. Was it worse to let him believe that I cheated or tell him the truth? Either way, he wouldn't support my new persona. I wasn't "innocent" anymore. My reputation was blasted into space. Overnight I became the most notorious freak show on campus. Who knew the suckers at school read online magazines? I wasn't Kat anymore, I was Groupie Kat. I had a title. I had a band name. I was an icon.

Charlie would ruin my fun. *Good riddance*, I thought. He would ask questions. I couldn't keep a straight face with him. I cared about him too much. The others were easy to bluff since they didn't know me. They lived for the gossip. They didn't care what I did or how I felt as long as they could be associated with a legend. Or, legend-fucker.

I reaped the rewards. I was the center of attention. The center of the universe. Ashley declared me her "BFF" so Madeline was obliged to play along. They showered me with unwarranted compliments.

"Kat, I love your jeans."

"Thanks? They were my dad's."

"Ooh, vintage."

It felt like I'd been wrung through a propaganda machine. Everything boring about me was suddenly fascinating. My irrelevance turned important. My obscurity became crucial. My opinions were coveted, sought-after, and fought over. "Kat, what do you think of this?" "What do you think of that?" "Let's ask Kat." My cheeks ached from talking so much.

How many days can the best day of my life last?

Nosebleed gave me rides to and from school. It happened suddenly and without reason. Monday afternoon he asked if I wanted a ride home and after the ride home he said, "I'll scoop you tomorrow morning." After that, he kept doing it.

The preppy kids weren't nice to me—they weren't even nice to each other—*but* the girls whispered and the boys called me names in the hallway. Death stares followed me everywhere. That meant I "made it" in their world. Being a slut was the most punk thing a punk girl could do. It was also the preppiest thing a preppy girl could do.

I didn't feel guilty. I wasn't telling lies, I was avoiding the truth. Everyone could believe what they wanted. No fake details passed my lips. My mouth stayed shut to let them dream. I was giving them the gift of fantasy. What they came up with was better than what I'd say anyway.

The problem was my virginity. If I was not careful, the truth would spill. Whoever I dated next would expect me to be a sex goddess. I decided this was my last chance: that weekend I *had to* do it with Bob. Just get it over with. There was no way in hell he read *Gunshot*. I doubt he ever surfed the net.

After school I asked Nosebleed to drop me off at Chapel Hill Comics. I was too anxious to wait for Saturday. "I guess," he said, accepting my request. Nosebleed blasted the Dead Boys so loud it didn't matter we had nothing to say. I figured he was contemplating. Getting used to being alone with me. To me being as cool as him, unexpectedly. Maybe cooler. He raced on small roads with fifteen-miles-per-hour speed limits. We flew over speed bumps. I tried not to think about all the deer trying to cross the street. I tried not to think about Charlie.

SCR E E E EEE*CH!*

Nosebleed halted and I hopped out. He blew away as I waved. Bob looked shocked at my arrival.

"Kat on a school day?"

"I'm shaking things up."

"I'd say so."

"What's new?" he asked innocuously. I studied his face. It was hard to tell what he knew.

"I got a gift for you."

"Again?"

"This one's from Japan. I think it's illegal in most countries." He handed me a brown paper bag taped shut.

"Thanks, dude." I shoved it in my bag.

"Do you have time to read now that you're famous?"

"Oh, God." I banged my head against the counter dramatically.

"You didn't think I go online? How lame do I look?"

"Pretty lame." I kept my head on the counter. *Maybe if I slam my head hard enough into the glass and bleed everywhere I can end this conversation.*

"I'm not here to criticize." He lowered his head down next to mine. "I'm here to gossip."

"That's a relief," I said sarcastically.

"So, what happened?"

"What happened was I had a good time!" I exclaimed, defeated. I stood up and he did, too. The world was sweeter from the perspective of the counter. I should have stayed there. Standing up felt like a smack in the face, like leaving a movie theater to see the sun went down while you were inside.

"Kat, come on. I can't believe I'm friends with a groupie."

"Who said I'm your friend." My voice followed me outside. Dammit. Was there a person in the world who didn't read the story? I walked home in a stupor.

The internet has gone too far. Punk's not dead but print is. The internet strangled it. That's why the bookstore has no customers. Nah, the bookstore has no customers because they sell weird books nobody likes. And you're bad at your job. But the internet has gone too far. What can you do about it? Nothing. You just need to survive. Don't reveal your lie. Lose your virginity. Kill your audition. You'll get into music school and next year you'll be gone. It's no big deal. You were born to do this.

Practice begged to differ. I was a disaster. Playing felt draining. My hands weren't listening to the books or my brain. Frustrated tears burned my cheeks. The *Minute Waltz* took an hour. It was pointless. I was done. Finished.

I punched the keys.

SLAM

Bang !

Smash.

I ran upstairs and opened Bob's gift. Manga I'd never heard of. *Take On Me.*

There was a half-naked girl on the cover. Manga is read from the back cover (as we know it) to the front. The word bubbles and actions are read from right to left, in a series of three. Start at the top right, go one left, then down. Then bottom right, move left, then down.

This wasn't manga. This was hentai. Porn. I heard this stuff was big in Japan but never saw it for myself. I couldn't understand the Japanese but anyone could grasp the story. From skimming the pages I could tell it was about a schoolgirl getting her brains screwed out all over town. It was gruesome. Bob was right, this was probably illegal in some countries. Surely in North Carolina. I was probably breaking a law just by holding it, having it, hiding it in my room. *Why did he give this to me?*

I wondered, putting my hand down my pants.

SOUTHPOINT MALL

Friday morning I sat on the curb waiting for Nosebleed. *Unbelievable. Last week you were a school bus girl. A different Kat, completely. Do the school bus kids miss you? Who sits in the back now? They leave my spot empty, as a sign of respect.* Diving into ego masturbation, I got a text from Ashley.

"SKIP 2DAY. Meet @ southpoint fountain"

"Nosebld taking me 2 school," I texted.

"HE'LL DRIVE U 2 S-POINT!" she replied.

I figured he'd refuse so I could tell Ashley that we'll shoplift another day. Like, over the weekend. Like, when normal high school girls shoplift.

Nosebleed blasted onto my street. He appeared out of nowhere, as if from another dimension. I hopped into his wagon.

"'Sup, Kat," he barked over the Adicts.

"Hey, Nosebleed," I yelled. "Ashley just texted. She wants to meet at Southpoint. That's nuts, right?"

"I'll take you," he shouted. "We'll stop for biscuits."

Shit. "Thanks, dude. You don't have to."

He turned the music up more and roared. "Nothing better to do."

What about school? Are you the only loser who cares? Nosebleed cared. He ate his biscuit on the way to Southpoint, stopped in the parking lot, and said get out. "Thanks." I coughed into the dust he left behind.

Ashley didn't know the Southpoint Fountain is the fountain where I met Josh. I tried not to think about him too much anymore but I couldn't not think about him when someone mentioned that fountain. When they'd say, "Southpoint Fountain," I completed the sentence in my head, Southpoint Fountain . . . *where I met Josh.* My heart ached for him as I waited. I put my butt in the exact spot it was in when I sat next to him that day. I wondered if I could summon him. He'd come out from the fountain and say, *Hey, sugar pie—*

"Hey, bitch." Ashley showed up late, skipping like a kid. "Come on," she snorted, as if *she* were the one waiting. As if she were the one whose chest ached with love . . . and leftover mosh pit bruising.

"I'm about to change your wardrobe *and* your life." It sounded like something she'd planned to say on the way. I was happy to think she planned anything for me.

We started at Victoria's Secret and worked our way around the mall. She taught me to go into the changing room with tons of stuff, load clothes under your clothes, and walk out wearing them. What didn't fit under your clothes could fit in your bag.

I only had my school backpack, full of books. Not much room for loot. "Next time bring an empty bag," she lectured, rolling her eyes.

She taught me *not* to avoid the salespeople. "Smile at them. *Act normal.*" Whatever that meant. She was miles away from normal.

She taught me about sensors. Which ones are okay to rip and which ones start an alarm or blow ink everywhere. She taught me how to keep watch.

"Once you're out of the store, they can't get you."

The top secret to shoplifting? Be a pretty white girl. Nobody paid attention to us, even though we dressed weird and acted sketchy.

"*Run, Kat. Run!*"

I ran all the way to the food court clutching my bag to my chest.

"Kat? Where are you going?"

"You told me to run." I turned around, panting.

"Not that far, you freak."

My heart stopped racing at the Cinnabon. I watched Ashley demolish a gooey bun with dense syrup. She didn't offer me any, fortunately. As she chewed I ran the day's scenes through my head, in awe of myself. Terror and euphoria flooded my body. *Kat: groupie and shoplifter. What can't she do?*

I got: two thongs, a bra I'd never wear, and a pair of tights.

Ashley got: a couple of Dior lip glosses, a handful of Victoria's Secret thongs, a Juicy Couture tracksuit, a fake fur coat from Lucky, a dress from Express, a shirt and a belt from Hot Topic.

I felt close to Ashley for a moment and wanted to ask her a personal question or give her a compliment or reach out and grab her hand, but I stopped myself. Intimacy is the death of friendship. Friendships last longer in the freezer. That way they can never curdle.

We rode the bus to her place. She lived in the Royal Park apartments. The name must be a joke made by the landlord. Her place was grimy and gray. The carpets were soiled and the ceiling was bumpy—a bad sign, Mom taught me. There was a black leather couch and a coffee table smothered in trash. It looked like a bachelor pad.

"*Mom?*" Ashley yelled. No answer. "Thank God."

She led me to her bedroom and slammed the door. On her bed she unloaded her loot. She took all of her clothes off. I turned away and she was like, "What are you doing?" So I turned back around and watched her.

Her body was astonishing. Her form belonged in Rome, a marble statue with fountains soaking her thighs. Her vagina looked different from mine. The inside parts stuck out. The hair above it was shaved into a heart shape. I wondered how Dexter could live with himself knowing his dirty hands touched her. I wondered what it's like to walk around with her body. I wondered if I was staring.

"Thoughts?" She packed herself into the Juicy Couture tracksuit. "Obviously I'd wear this ironically." She pulled her new thong so it poked out of the pants.

"Obviously." She wore it better than Paris Hilton.

"Try on your stuff."

"I only got underwear."

"Lame."

"Have you ever gotten caught?" I asked meekly.

"Only dumbasses get caught." She tore the tracksuit off and slipped into the Express dress. "Are you a dumbass?"

I dodged the question. "Your mom doesn't mind?"

"What?"

I pointed to her walls. They were covered in spray-painted Anarchy symbols, "ACAB," a dick, smiley faces with crossed-out eyes, and an upside-down cross.

"She's not allowed in my room."

"Rad."

"I'm gonna dye my hair wanna help?"

"Sure."

"We can do yours, too."

"I'm . . . not allowed to dye my hair."

"Says who?"

"My parents?"

"Well . . . if you do it *here* they can't stop you."

"But they'll be mad."

"And?"

"I don't want them to be."

"They're *parents*. They're supposed to be mad."

"I guess."

"Will they make you shave your head?"

"Nah."

"A buzz cut would be better than *that*." She pointed to my brown bob. "You've gotta do something with your hair. You can't be a redhead, obviously. But I've got a box of black dye." The way she grinned meant I had no choice.

I sat on the toilet as she worked over the sink. She had plastic gloves, salon brushes, and a bowl for mixing developer. She did most of her hair herself but I helped with the back. Each strip of hair had to be carefully brushed through, with special attention to the roots. When I was done my hands were bloodred. We covered her head in a plastic shopping bag. Then it was my turn.

She pulled a box from under the sink. Féria by L'Oréal. When I was a kid I sent L'Oréal a letter. I had drawn about a hundred baby seals on it, they were all crying with big cartoon tears. Some of them were holding signs that read DON'T TEST ON ME and STOP HURTING US. They sent me a letter back saying they don't test their products on seals.

The girl on the box was pretty in the dead-girl way. You've seen them, the girls in ads who aren't *real* models, who don't do runway or magazines? You just know they got their picture taken in some filthy room in some crappy building in some third-world country. She had neon eyes and jet-black hair with a blue shine. How mine was supposed to look.

The dye smelled delicious. I always enjoyed chemical smells. My favorite smell was gasoline. Especially in Dad's garage. Rubber cement came in second. Then markers, paint, and any kind of glue. She slathered the goo on my skull. I sat on the toilet in silence. Once my head was in a bag we made coffee. She smoked a few cigarettes.

"You smoke at home?" I wondered aloud.

"Why wouldn't I?"

Every day I learned new ways in which I wasn't cool.

A timer went off and she showered. She got out and made me get in. I took my clothes off warily, hoping she wouldn't watch me. She did, mercifully silent. Black water drained from under me. Like that scene in *Psycho*.

My transformation was dazing. I was severe and mature. Like a young Joan Jett.

My ears were black, too.

"Will that go away?" I asked.

"Duh. Do you love it?"

"Duh."

In my bedroom I listened to Thelonious Monk and thought of the first time I made Mom cry. In fourth grade we were putting on a play set in "pilgrim times." We were expected to costume ourselves. Mom made a delightful polka-dotted dress. I was elated.

We had an "old-fashioned" day in class before putting on the play. Mom packed a tin lunch box with a lard and pepper sandwich and a strudel. I merrily swung the box as I walked to school in my dress.

Marissa Craine, my friend at the time, laughed when I walked in. She was the only girl in our grade who already shaved her legs. She was platinum blonde with bloated lips and a year-round tan. She was like, "You can't do the play looking like that." She pulled another outfit out of her backpack. "Put this on." It wasn't old-fashioned, just a blue silky dress. It smelled like perspiration.

From the stage, I saw Mom. Disappointment distorted her features. All evening she wiped tears away.

When she walked me home, I asked, "Why are you mad at me?"

She said, "I didn't know you cared so much what other people think."

Mom looked at me the same way the afternoon I got back from Ashley's. That day, I didn't care. It was Friday and I was going to debut my new look at Dexter's.

PEPPER'S PIZZA

Nighttime was rarely mine. Walking in the dark felt like walking into the future. Alleys and parking lots looked marvelous in the dusk. Everyone was cool when lit up by moonlight and streetlights. I caught my reflection in windows. Nocturnal Kat was a wild street kid, free of parents and full of plans.

Mom thought I was meeting Lucy at Pepper's Pizza. She dropped me there so I walked to Dexter's. The blocks leading up to the Lab always made my heart pound. I held a key to the bright secret of our town. I sped up, toward the portal to fun.

When I reached the doorstep I stopped. Something within kept me from advancing. Usually the sight of Dexter's door intoxicated me with anticipation. That night, dread paralyzed me. My status there felt flimsy, up in the air. It felt like I was there for the first time. The first time with my secret. What would I tell Charlie? Could I dodge Dexter's jokes? Brush off the teasing? Would they gang up on me? Interrogate me?

Worship me? Which was worse? Ashley, Madeline, and Nosebleed were easy to fool. But those guys? No chance. I was in for a scandal. Mayhem, madness, murder.

You can tell the truth, Kat. Let it out now, before it's too late. "Just kidding, I'm a virgin." Rip it off, like a Band-Aid. "Not a groupie, just a fan." Just do it. Laugh it off. "Journalists, am I right?" Humiliating. You'd rather die, let's face it. Roll with the punches. Take the truth to your grave. Don't snitch on yourself.

With a deep breath I stepped in, surrendering to my fate.

Jeremy was in the hallway, trying to punch a hole in the wall next to another hole in the wall. I hadn't seen him in forever. On September eleventh (yes, that one) I missed the school bus and ended up walking all the way to school. When I wandered in everything was quiet. Then I saw Jeremy running around. He sprinted to me and shook my shoulders, yelling, "*Anarchy! Anarchy!*" Which wasn't that different than usual. But he was alone in the halls, banging on all the lockers. It was eerie. I was like, "What's up, Jeremy?"

"The Twin Towers just got attacked. It's war. It's anarchy."

"What do you mean?"

"I mean two airplanes just flew into the fucking Twin Towers."

"What's the Twin Towers?"

"Just—forget it. *Anarchy in the USA*!"

He ran off and I went to class and saw the television. Everyone was freaking out. I couldn't see much from the screen. Some people falling out of buildings. They made us all do the Pledge of Allegiance. I didn't stand up for it. Liberty Spike Ben sat it out with me. We called him that because he had liberty spikes, like the Statue of Liberty. Mr. Stevens usually liked Ben and me but that day he didn't and he didn't any day after that.

"Cool hole," I said, as Jeremy pulled his hand out of the wall.

He admired his bloody knuckles. "'Sup, Kat?"

"Nothing. Haven't seen you in forever."

"I just got back from wilderness camp," he proudly announced.

"What's wilderness camp?"

"Remember when I went to juvie?"

"Of course." Jeremy going to a juvenile detention center was the coolest thing that happened to any of us in middle school. It was cooler than when I got suspended. He totally overshadowed me.

"It's like juvie but way intense. I got kidnapped one night and taken to the woods. It was like the army. We had to sleep outside and do drills. They starved us."

"Wait. *Who* kidnapped you?"

"My mom. I mean, she hired them to do it."

"Whoa. That's fucked-up."

"It's all right. Congrats on fucking Trippy Dope." He opened the fridge door and disappeared behind it. *What the shit.* Jeremy was in the woods. How did *he* know? I glared at the fridge door. My gateway to wonder turned against me. Everyone behind that fridge door told Jeremy. They were all sitting there, talking about me. Gossiping. I wanted to throw up. I couldn't follow Jeremy into the Party Room. Maybe a minute ago I had a chance but he shook me. I had too much bad energy shooting in every wrong direction. I directed the energy toward the kitchen. I opened the real refrigerator and grabbed a beer. Someone tapped me on the shoulder. I stood up and saw Jake.

"Hey," he said. "You look different."

"Hey, yeah, hair." He wore the same outfit I saw him in last time. He smelled like coffee, like last time. He looked perfect, like last time. I was sad he hadn't called me.

"Sorry I never called."

"It's cool."

"I heard you were Charlie's girl. I didn't wanna interfere."

"I'm not anymore."

"I heard."

"What else have you heard?"

Shit, Kat, why'd you ask that?

My body heat turned up to a thousand degrees. As I burned, time froze. Millennia passed as Jake blinked. I counted his eyelashes and talked myself out of spiraling into paranoia. *You aren't lying. Boys tell lies, girls keep secrets. This secret is an act of rebellion. An assertion of defiance. You're claiming the gossip of generations of women before you. You're letting it serve rather than hurt you. You're radical and radically sensitive. You control your narrative.*

"What do you mean?" The fourth dimension returned to normal.

Relief soaked me like iced tea. "Nothing. Want a beer?"

"Nah, let's get out of here."

"I just got here."

"It's just the usual scumbags and dickheads."

"I've been waiting all week to hang out with those scumbags and dickheads."

"Eh." He shrugged.

"And besides, I just opened my beer," I added, opening my beer.

"You can drink it in my car."

But you have so much to do tonight. Debut your new hair and bad reputation. Smooth things over with Charlie. Impress Dexter with your story. Revamp your social life. Then again, tonight could be your destruction. Charlie and Dexter would water-torture you until you confess your truth. A virgin. A liar. They'll humiliate you. Maybe Jake came here to rescue me . . . why else would he be so persistent?

"What else is going on?" I asked.

"We'll make our own fun."

He knows what's coming. He heard them talking shit. They're planning an attack and he's disrupting it. He's saving your life. You hit the jackpot. A night out with Jake and you can avoid the truth and the lies and let this blow over.

"Let's ditch this dump." I was conquered.

Crisis averted.

We got out before anyone could sniff me out. They'd think I never showed up in the first place. Only Jeremy saw me and nobody trusted Jeremy, not even before he lost his mind in the wild.

Jake's car looked like a toy car. It was the kind of red that only a car can be. Not cherry red or Valentino red or Ashley's hair red. Car Red. The headlights came up like eyes. His rearview mirror was held together with duct tape. The interior fabric was decorated in various stains. It smelled of stale smoke and spilled booze. The perfect beat-up-deadbeat ride.

We listened to Elliott Smith and cruised all over town. We'd pick a neighborhood, drive down each street, including dead ends and cul-de-sacs. Once we explored it all we'd pick a spot to park, have a smoke there, and go off to find another neighborhood.

When we ran out of neighborhoods we circled downtown ten times. College students wearing Carolina blue packed Franklin Street, wasted. They behaved worse than the punks.

Hours passed and we didn't say much. The silence with him was comfortable. He held my hand in his lap. Chapel Hill looked different from my passenger window. More dazzling and dreamy.

He parked in front of the Rape Crisis Center.

"I've done community service here," I said.

"Let's make out here," he said, pulling me in by the back of the neck. He didn't slobber like some boys did. A no-nonsense kisser. He always smelled like coffee and now I knew he tasted like it. I pulled away, for a breath.

"That was weird, sorry." He cackled. "I just thought it would be funny to make out at the Rape Crisis Center."

"I can see how that's funny." I couldn't see how that was funny.

"Wanna go to a movie?"

"I think the theaters are closed."

"I mean tomorrow."

"Oh, yeah, duh."

"It's late. Where do you live?"

He drove me home and eyed the stairs leading to my door. "I'd walk you up but that might be too much."

"No worries."

He kissed me and said, "I had fun with you."

"Me too."

"Too bad you have a curfew."

I eyed the car clock: 11:32. "I've actually got half an hour."

"Ah, well, I need to head back to the party."

"You're going back to Dexter's?" The shock in my voice was profound.

"There's nothing else to do."

I slid out of the car, hiding my bewilderment. I was hurt that he was going back without me. I leaned into his window from the outside, like a hooker. I decided to be cool. Questions are not cool.

"Have fun."

"I will." He sped off, to enjoy my friends without me.

Don't be jealous of Jake. He saved your life. Maintained your dignity. Kept you from disgrace. Plus, he wanted you alone. You should be happy. Honored. You got to kiss your new crush! Your next boyfriend? Don't worry about those dipshits and dirt bags, or whatever he called them . . . you'll enjoy the party next weekend. By then everyone will forget your mess. Dexter isn't going anywhere.

I spun that in my head until I convinced myself it was true or fell asleep, whichever came first. I woke up light, my memories of the night glossed into a glittery music video. *He kissed me. HE kissed me. He kissed ME. He KISSED me.* I cruised through my bookstore duties and flirted fluently with Bob. I didn't mention the porno he gave me. He finally asked me out.

"You wanna watch a movie at mine?"

Losing my virginity to Bob was still my best bet. Jake could find out the gossip any minute and expect me to be a seductress. Maybe he already knew and was playing it cool? No way, he would have said something, like everyone else did. Still, time wasn't on my side. So it was decided. Bob would get it first. No matter what he expected or if I'd disappoint him. I didn't care what Bob thought of me.

"I've got plans tonight, how's next Saturday?"

"You're booked all week? Damn."

"I can't go out on school nights. Weekends only, unless there's a concert."

"Got it. Strict European parents. That's hot."

"Yeah, right."

"Come in after your shift Saturday. We'll close up here then go to mine."

"I've got piano after my shift. We can meet up after?"

"Whatever, never mind." He turned around and started organizing the stacks behind the counter. I stood there for a second, waiting for him to say something, like, "Give me your number," or, "We'll figure it out next week." When I realized that wouldn't happen, I walked out, unnoticed.

Aren't older guys supposed to be mature?

My piano teacher tore angrily through ten Altoids. He covered my books in red ink and made me improvise jazz forever. I was too embarrassed by my playing to bring up the recommendation letter. I figured I can just type it up myself and have him sign it . . . or forge his signature. Or give up completely and run away and find Josh.

I felt sick when I got home. I couldn't keep down a grilled cheese. I showered, plucked my eyebrows, and put an outfit together for Jake. My red tennis skirt, black opaque tights, a little boy's button-down shirt, Dad's jacket, and combat boots. I threw on heavy eyeliner and lip gloss. Underneath it all I had on a thong I shoplifted with Ashley. I had to wash it discreetly by hand so Mom wouldn't ask where it came from.

When I saw his red car I felt relief. Jake didn't come upstairs to meet my parents.

He just honked. Mom shook her head. Dad waved from the garage. "Your dad looks like Popeye," he said when I got to the car.

"I love Popeye." I buckled my seat belt.

"Do you love your dad?" He sped off.

"Of course." I rolled down the window.

"You're lucky," he said. Then paused, begging to be asked . . .

"Do *you* . . . love your dad?"

"He abandoned us and lives in a trailer drinking himself to death."

"Oh. I'm sorry."

"He's funny. I'll introduce y'all." He turned up the music, which signaled us both to be quiet. Conversations that lasted more than a few minutes seemed to exhaust him. "Bone Machine" was playing. Jake had good taste, he didn't only listen to punk. He liked moody stuff. The Pixies, the Smiths,

Ratatat, Joy Division, and the Cure. He also randomly loved Jimi Hendrix, which didn't make sense.

We went to the Varsity Theatre on Franklin. It was a small theater with old green carpets and stairs that creek when you step on them. The Varsity has only two screens showing one old and one new movie. We saw a new one, *Nói Albanói*. A foreign film, Icelandic, probably. It's about a boy who falls in love with a girl in a small frozen town. He tries to convince her to move away with him, somewhere tropical. Before they can, a storm kills everyone.

I cried at the end and he squeezed my hand.

"How was the rest of the party?" I asked at the Cold Stone Creamery. I tried to sound nonchalant. I made sure to wait until after the film to bring it up.

"Let's see . . . Nosebleed pierced his nose *and* Madeline's nose. Little Tim beat up a methhead, and . . . Dexter puked everywhere."

"Damn, I missed out." I carefully licked my cookie dough ice cream and wondered how to casually ask about Charlie. "Did you see Charlie?" I blurted.

"Charlie was all over some rockabilly girl with a big butt."

"Who? How big is her butt?" I asked jokingly, but seriously wanted to know.

"I don't know, I can't stand rockabilly chicks. She looked like they all do. Curled bangs, pinup dress, letterman jacket . . . stupid."

He didn't tell me how big her butt was. "If you have nothing to say, scream."

"Huh?"

"You know, people say, 'If you have nothing nice to say, don't say anything at all?' It's a good concept, but practically impossible. I think it's hard to stay silent in the moment you want to say something negative. But at the same time, you want to avoid saying something negative, because it isn't good energy. So, if you have nothing nice to say, scream."

"All right." Jake finished his ice cream.

I didn't scream but I wanted to.

We drove to the gas station by Rosemary Street. A crackhead hung out there waiting for needy kids. We gave him extra bucks to buy us beer. He also bought kids cigarettes but Jake was nineteen and old enough to get them himself. I flipped through the celebrity gossip magazines while Jake got smokes and snacks. *Us Weekly* and *People* were my favorites. "I feel bad for celebrity kids," I said, staring at paparazzi pictures of Madonna's daughter.

"What?"

"They're set up for failure. If they go into entertainment they'll never be as good as their parents. If they *are* good, nobody will give them credit. They'll always be someone's kid. And if they choose to sit back and do nothing they're hated for *that*. Everyone resents them just for being born."

"I can't believe you read that shit," he said.

"Just for fun," I muttered, slipping the mag back into her slot. Trashy papers were my purest pleasure. I wished my bookstore carried them. Fashion magazines, too. They reminded me that the world was bigger than Chapel Hill. Countless streets around the world had their own versions of the cart lady, the guy with baby doll heads stuck all over his car, Crazy Pete and the crackhead who buys kids beer. I bet they had their own versions of me, too.

We sat on the hood of the car drinking from paper bags. I spotted Lucy walking toward us and hid behind Jake.

"What are you doing?" he said.

"Avoiding someone."

"Do I need to fuck them up?" He looked around stoically.

"It's not like that," I whispered. "It's a girl."

"I'm not sexist." He laughed. "Equal rights equal fights."

"Haha . . . she's harmless."

Lucy walked into the gas station with two preps from school. The kind that got good grades and had rich parents. The kind who threw big parties I was never invited to. Not that I would have gone if I were. What did they even talk about? Britney's benders and Lilo's weight loss? When I couldn't see her anymore I revealed myself. "They look lame," Jake said. "Let's go."

"To Dexter's?" I tested.

"Nah. Let's be alone."

"Okay." I sighed.

"What's wrong?"

"Nothing."

"You wanna go to Dexter's?" He slid off the hood.

"Yeah, but no, I see most of them at school anyway."

"I can't believe you're still in school." He unlocked the car and got in.

"I mean, I'm sixteen." I hopped in next to him.

"You could drop out." He sped off.

"I could, yeah. I hate school. But from next year I'll be in Winston-Salem. Music school. I'm gonna graduate there."

"Why would you do that?"

"For piano. To get away. To be with artists. So I never have to study math again or change into gym clothes around a bunch of bitches. A million reasons."

"Damn."

"My audition's in April. I hope I get in."

"I hope you don't."

"The fuck?" I hit him playfully on the shoulder.

"If you go there, how will I see you?"

That made me blush. We drove into a dark neighborhood and parked in front of a house. "This will be my place soon," he said, getting out of the car.

I got out and stretched. "It's nice."

"Yeah, well, not that part." He gestured toward the house. "I'm gonna live in *there*." He turned and pointed to a shed in the backyard. "I'll get to use the kitchen and bathroom in the main house, but pay less. And this way it's like I've got my own spot, you know?"

"Hell yeah. Who lives in the main house?"

"A vegan butcher and a . . . salesman."

"Sick. When do you move in?"

"As soon as I get some cash together."

"Congrats," I said, gazing at the shed.

I looked over and caught him gazing at me. I was like, "What?"

"You're so graceful."

"Huh?"

"You aren't harsh, like Ashley. You're elegant. Like a ballerina."

I hated when guys complimented one girl by insulting other girls. Implying that being unlike other girls meant you were good, because other girls were bad. Also, fuck ballerinas. "Thanks. But I can be harsh, too."

"I just wanted to be nice." He got back in the car and I followed.

"Sorry, compliments embarrass me."

"Another thing I like about you."

"Jeez."

"Look at the time," he exclaimed, seeing the car clock at 11:48. "I gotta take Cinderella home before she becomes pumpkin pie."

"That's not how it goes," I said.

"We can find out. I'll hold you hostage."

"No." I laughed. "Take me home."

"Okay, tonight I will. But when I have my own place . . . I'll keep you."

"Oh, yeah? Even if I'm a pumpkin pie?"

"I love pie."

I didn't ask if he was going to Dexter's after. I knew he would.

CAFFÉ DRIADE

Ashley and I skipped on Monday. I lifted a plaid miniskirt from Time After Time, a dog collar from Light Years, and a bowling shirt from Nice Price Books. Ashley lifted enough to open her own shop. We stayed downtown, away from the mall. She said she skips around when shoplifting, so the fuzz ain't on her tail. We went to Cosmic Cantina for lunch, where she got tacos and I had Diet Coke. She was like, "Do you ever hear from Trippy?"

I shrugged. "He's busy." She seemed disappointed so I told her that I made out with Jake.

She perked up. "So *that's* why you ditched us this weekend."

"I didn't mean to. He sort of kidnapped me."

"I told them. I was like, Kat's too busy being a harlot to hang." She tilted her head back and laughed.

"We'll probably have sex soon." I poured gas on her fire.

"Good for you. I have a thing for Jake."

"For real?"

"Don't worry, Dexter would *slaughter me* if I cheated on him. He's really intense. We were fighting once and I said I'd dump him and he said he'd murder-suicide if I did." She laughed. "He can't live without me."

"How often do you guys do it?"

"If I weren't on the pill I'd have a hundred babies."

"Your babies would be cute."

"Ew, Kat." She scrunched up her face.

"I just mean you're cute. So is Dexter. But I say that in a platonic way."

"Yeah. Dexter's the hottest guy in town. Jake is second hottest."

Ashley walked fast and I paced behind her. I liked watching her walk and watching other people watch her. Ashley was powerful. Girls like her held remarkable force. Whether they knew it and accepted it or not wasn't relevant. Hot Girl Power isn't the kind one can enjoy or sustain independently. Hot Girl Power demands an audience, a consumer. The girls who have the Power can't refuse it or control it. Nobody lets them.

People happily submit to Big Man Power because they respect it. They nourish it and it flourishes. Big Man Power gets stronger with time, with age. Hot Girl Power peaks when a girl is young and vanishes soon after. Men make sure of that. The exquisite feminine scares them, so they squash it. First they get a taste, a piece of the pie. But they don't stop there. They steal, dig, and devour it until it's used up, gone, demolished.

Men on the street wanted Ashley and hated her for it. Because what they wanted from her wasn't nice. They didn't want to be accepted or loved by her. They wanted to command her. Annihilate her so they were no longer powerless around her.

Ashley walked on, bursting with Hot Girl Power. Omnipotent and out of her hands. Ultimately she'd suffer for the Power, or its eventual absence. Still, I would have died, sacrificed everything I love, given up piano and all my CDs, just to experience it, even for a second.

"Kat, catch up," she huffed.

"Coming." I scuttled.

Charlie was back at school on Tuesday. He avoided me in every way possible. First, he dodged my eyes on the hill. When I spoke to him he didn't answer, even in front of everyone. He acted like I wasn't there. When I approached him in the hallway he turned and walked away. It was awful. His scorn stung unbearably. I missed his friendship. I missed not being a villain. It didn't matter anymore that the whole school thought I was cool. Charlie was the victim, the moral compass and mirror to my soul. The mirror said: you're superficial. Charlie thinking I cheated on him with Trippy was bad.

Letting him continue to believe that in order to serve my image was worse. Not reaching out to him until now was crap. My guilt projectile vomited all over everything. I couldn't handle it.

I skipped the rest of the week. Nosebleed drove me to Caffé Driade every morning. Jake worked at Caffé Driade. That's why he smelled like coffee. I could hang out there all day and have whatever I wanted, for free. I was hopped up on black coffee, San Pellegrino, and Marlboro Reds (bummed from Jake). On an empty stomach, usually.

I did homework and read comics while Jake served customers. He hated all of them. He made it obvious, scoffing at their needs. As far as he was concerned, the only acceptable orders were: black coffee, straight espresso, or a classic cappuccino (short, tight foam, ceramic cup, single shot, unsweetened, whole milk, with no exceptions and absolutely *no* syrup flavoring). Few customers lived up to his expectations. Sometimes he'd make me hot chocolate but he didn't judge me for it because he knew that by then I was one coffee away from a seizure.

When a friend came in he'd hold up the line by talking them up. Then, when it seemed the conversation was over, that he may be ready for the next client, he'd say "Be right back" and go outside to smoke. People would sigh, gasp, throw their hands up, curse, complain . . . but they stayed put, waiting for Jake. Because they needed him.

Because he was the best.

He also knew how to work a register.

One evening I watched him close. He took out the trash, washed the dishes, stacked the chairs on the tables, swept the floor. Then he took the money out of the register, counted it, and wrote stuff down in a big book. He separated the money into two paper bags. He put one bag in a drawer under the sink. He put another bag into his backpack. "What's that?" I asked. "Coffee," he said. I didn't ask again. After work he went out and I went home. I thought about him all the time, more than I thought about Josh. He didn't call me like Josh did, he said he preferred "the real thing."

Friday night Jake took me to his new place. It had no heat, no lights, no furniture.

It smelled like a shed because it was a shed. He said, "Welcome to my love shack." We sat on a blanket on the floor. He got us a bottle of André, to celebrate. He was like, "I used all my cash on the down payment. But next week I'll get a bed and power." I said, "Awesome." We finished the bottle and kissed a little, in silence. It wasn't the right setting for sex, he knew that. But the following week he'd expect it, if he had a new bed and everything.

When it got dark we went into the main house, which was a relief, since I had to pee. His shed didn't have a toilet. I met the roommates. Damon was a frail dude who worked as a butcher at Weaver Street, even though he was vegan. I asked him, is your job difficult for you? He was like, why would it be? The other guy, Maron, was bearded and barefoot, in soiled hippie clothes.

When Jake drove me home I couldn't help asking. "*That's* the salesman? What does he sell, Hacky Sacks?"

"Funny, Kat. He sells dope."

"Weed?"

"No."

Pause.

"So?"

Jake sighed, annoyed. "You know the Velvet Underground song, 'Waiting for the Man'?"

"Of course."

"He's the man."

TIME-OUT

Time-Out united everyone: sorority girls, frat boys, professors, dropouts, blue collars, white collars, dog collars, punks, preps, bimbos, junkies, PhDs, immigrants, tourists, townies, stoners, soccer wives, horny dads, hookers, cops, criminals, Christians, crackheads, hairdressers, and hobos. They didn't have grilled cheese, just southern comfort food served cafeteria style. Fried chicken, mashed potatoes, biscuits, grits, collard greens, sweet tea, pecan pie. Everyone loved it because it was cheap, easy, and always open. Even at midnight on Christmas.

Bob got mashed potatoes with gravy. I tried not to gag watching him chew food that didn't need chewing. "A fat girl asked me on a date." He stammered, "I don't know if I should go."

"Why wouldn't you? Because she's fat?" I picked at my biscuit.

"No, she's cute. But she seems boring."

"How so?"

"Like, uninteresting?" Gravy clung to the side of his mouth.

"Not into comic books?" I teased.

"Hmm . . . I see your point."

"Go on the date."

"You're telling me to go on a date while on a date with me?"

"What's the big deal? I'm also seeing someone."

"Trippy Dope?"

"Stop."

"Kidding. Anyway, you're too young to be on a date with me."

"You're right. We can't be seen together." I looked over my shoulder. "We should go to your place." I was paranoid, but not because of the age difference. What if Dexter popped in for a biscuit? What if Charlie stopped by for sweet tea? They all loved this place, even Ashley. For all I knew Jake was around the corner. If he caught me lying about plans it would be a disaster on top of my current social shitpile.

Eat up, fucker.

"What's the rush? I wanna show my underage groupie off." He gloated.

"Seriously? If you mention that again I'm out."

"I won't bring it up again . . . tonight."

I'd met Bob after my shift, like he wanted. I told Mom my piano teacher canceled lessons and told my piano teacher I was sick. I told Jake I was going to a movie with Mom. I told Mom I was going to a movie with Lucy. I needed a break, I needed a breakthrough, I needed to lose my virginity to Bob.

Bob finished his baby food and went to the toilet, where he must have noticed the gravy on his face, since he walked out without it. Was he glad I didn't tell him? Or embarrassed I let him keep it there so long? Would this ego death prevent him from getting it up? I wondered as he walked me home.

Bob lived in one of those classic Rosemary Street houses: brick walls and a triangle roof. Charming and snug, with wooden floors and peeling paint. The air was musky, like the windows hadn't been opened in too long. I was like, "Your roommates aren't home?" He told me he lived alone. I didn't know anyone who didn't have roommates or parents. Dexter didn't count, he was never home alone.

"Make yourself comfortable, I'll get drinks." He fumbled around the kitchen. I sat on the couch and turned on the TV. Static on every channel. "I only have a VCR," he called out. "Okay," I yelled, turning it off. The TV was surrounded by bookshelves, heavy with comics, bent wood barely supporting the weight of the books. A record player leaned against the opposite wall. An impressive collection of vinyl smothered the floor. So this is an adult apartment, I thought. Cool.

Bob came back with two cocktails, something brown. We clinked glasses and the ice sloshed around. I chugged mine and it burned my throat.

"You're supposed to sip this."

"I'm thirsty."

He watched me drink the rest of it. "You want another one?"

"I'm good. Let's watch a movie."

"What are you in the mood for?"

"I don't know, man. Just pick something." I was feeling bratty.

"Yes, ma'am." He got up and shuffled around in the bookshelf. "Do you like Adult Swim?"

"Love it."

"*Aqua Teen* or *Sealab*?"

"*Sealab*."

If you're lookin' for me, better check under the sea, 'cause that is where you'll find me, underneath the Sealab, underneath the water . . . The theme song soothed me. Bob sat down close and put his arm around my shoulders. It was incredibly awkward, like hugging your mailman randomly would be. But he smelled like laundry detergent and didn't seem sweaty, so I let myself lean into him. We got through half an episode before he kissed me. I lay back and he lay on top of me, pinning my hands above my head. I closed my eyes as he fumbled with my tights, pulling them down.

He kissed my neck while pulling nervously at my panties. He pushed them to the side and started poking me, rushed and thoughtless, like the boys did at the skate park.

His hand was brutish and clumsy. He seemed frustrated, so I moved my pelvis toward him, like, *Here, let me help you.* I wanted to get it over with.

"There you are," he sighed, sticking his finger inside me. It felt like inserting a super tampon, only too fast and too hard. "You're like a Cheerio," he breathed.

I looked up at his face and felt repulsed. I hated him.

"Whoa, what's wrong?"

My cheeks were flushed and wet. *Fuck, Kat, you're crying.*

I didn't know what was wrong. But if I did I wouldn't have told him.

"Sorry." I pushed him off. "I gotta go."

He looked crushed as I fled the couch. His mouth hung wide in disbelief.

"I'm sorry." I wiped my face, pulled my tights up, and headed toward the door. He didn't follow me. When I got out and breathed fresh air, I stopped crying. Just like that. I forgot about him immediately. Pushed it out of my mind.

I started walking home but after a few blocks realized I shouldn't. I'd have to make up too many lies to undo the lies I told earlier. I turned around, toward Dexter's Lab. I hadn't been there since the night Jake kissed me. An eternity had passed in a couple of weeks. I wasn't worried anymore, I was beyond that. Charlie hated me, I knew that. How much worse could it get? They could kick me out, if they wanted. In that case I'd go to Jake.

Oh, right, Jake. Should you text him? If you don't text him and he's at Dexter's and sees you there he'll want to know why you didn't text him. Having a boyfriend is exhausting. Is he your boyfriend? You don't owe him a text . . . he doesn't tell you everywhere he goes. Anyway it's best to avoid further drama.

I texted Jake, "Change of plans going 2 Dextrz."

I was wearing the outfit I wore to the bookstore that day: my new plaid mini, opaque tights, combat boots, a ratty hoodie, and Dad's jacket. I checked myself in a car mirror. Tears smeared mascara under my eyes. It looked cool. I dug lip gloss out of my purse and applied several layers. My black hair pulled the look together. I was ready for whatever.

Dexter's door was always unlocked but that night it was wide open. Like someone broke in and made a run for it when they saw there's nothing to rob. All my energy was consumed in acting as if *I* were normal, as if *I* weren't drowning, so I didn't think twice about the door. I just closed it behind me. The Dead Milkmen played sharply. The hallway and kitchen were empty. Weird. I opened the fridge door and stepped into the Party Room.

Dexter was smashed. Lying on the carpet, limbs spread in all directions.

"Where is everyone?" I asked, looking around. No sign of our crew. No skaters, skins, hobos, or dealers, either. Just Dexter and me.

He rolled his head to the side, drooled on the floor. The carpet was burned and decaying. I sat down and inhaled his stink. It made me feel at home. I asked if he had beer. He didn't answer. I said, "Ashley and I are tight now. She takes me lifting."

He didn't reply. I texted Ashley, "where r U? I'm @ ur BF."

She replied instantly. "COMING DAMMIT!"

"Ashley's on her way," I said to snoozing Dexter.

I'd never seen the Lab like this, so peaceful. My ringtone startled me. It was Jake.

"Hey," I answered cheerfully.

"You at the Lab?" His voice was urgent.

"Just got here."

"I'm in the bathroom."

"Oh, all right. I'm coming." I got up.

"No. I'm making Dexter a bath. Stay with him."

"You're what?" I sat down.

"Keep him conscious till I'm back."

Conscious? He hung up and I turned to Dexter. On closer scrutiny, he seemed more sick than usual. His skin was transparent and blue. "Dexter?" I shook him. "Dexter." I pulled up an eyelid and his eyeball rolled backwards.

"*Oh my God. Dexter wake up!*" I punched his arm, slapped his cheeks, and gripped a handful of his hair. He didn't react.

I called Jake and heard his ringtone from inside the bathroom. "He won't wake up. I'm calling an ambulance."

"Don't you dare, Kat. Just talk to him."

Jake hung up.

This is it, the end of your life. Dexter will die. You'll go to jail. Just like that, it's all over. Your life could have been different. You should have slept with Bob. You should have gone to piano. You could have stayed home.

"Dear God, who I don't believe in," I whispered, "if Dexter survives this and if I survive this I swear I will be good forever."

Jake rushed into the Party Room with Nosebleed. They ignored me, pulled Dexter up by the armpits, and dragged him down the hall to the bathroom. I followed but stopped at the bathroom door. The boys threw Dexter inside a cold bath with all his clothes on. I watched the water soak my favorite sweater and favorite pair of jeans. The fabric darkened as Dexter's skin brightened. He was a porcelain doll, preserved and pickled.

Little bubbles fluttered from his nose. His eyes shot open.

Ashley busted into the Lab, yelling, "Dexter! Where is he?"

"We're in here." I sounded troubled, like my mother.

She barged in, pushing me backwards. "He's *fine*?" she scoffed. "I got fired for this." She was wearing her work clothes.

Dexter sat up in the bath, resurrected. Drool and snot mixed with water.

"Nosebleed, give Dexter a shower," Jake instructed.

"Nah, that's gay," Nosebleed said.

"Dude, *prison* is gay. Give him a fucking shower."

Nosebleed laughed. Ashley was like, "I'll give my own boyfriend a fucking shower. You people are idiots." She hugged Dexter, soaking her uniform. "It's okay, baby, I'm here." He sputtered confused, bumbling nonsense.

The boys and I left the bathroom and shut the door behind us. Out of respect or embarrassment. We sat in the Party Room, dumbfounded.

"That was crazy," Nosebleed said.

"Yep," agreed Jake.

"What happened?" My voice cracked.

"Dexter OD'd," Jake explained, slack-jawed. The sparkle in his eyes was dimmed. He spoke slower. I pressed on.

"Where is everyone? It's Saturday night."

"They got freaked out." He shrugged.

"Because he OD'd?"

"Nah, before. They didn't wanna be around him shooting up."

"What do you mean?"

"I mean it freaked them out."

"No, I mean, what do you mean, *shooting up*."

"Kat, I'm tired. Don't make me explain what you already know."

Ashley told us to leave. Nosebleed said there's a show at Go! Studios. He offered us a ride. Jake said he sobered up and that we'd meet Nosebleed there. He changed his mind in the car and we ended up in some parking lot. He asked if I wanted to go to the backseat and I said sure. We started making out and taking our clothes off.

I knew what was coming. There was nothing else for us to do. You can't not have sex after seeing what we did. Life was too raw to pretend it wasn't. My nerves were so wrecked between what I witnessed at Dexter's and what happened with Bob, I couldn't even tell if I was nervous. I mean, I was, but not about my virginity. It didn't seem to matter.

It took him forever to get inside me. He was like, "I can stop if it hurts."

I was like, "It hurts but keep going."

"It won't go in."

"Push harder." The pain was immeasurable. Like being on fire. Tears streamed down my face but I wasn't *crying* crying. My eyes were passive faucets. In my head I played that song by the Boys, "First Time."

Oh . . . oh oh oh . . . it's my first time
Oh . . . oh oh oh . . . please be kind
Oh . . . oh oh oh . . . don't hurt me
Oh. . . . oh oh oh . . .
I didn't know what to say

Didn't want to hurt in any way
I looked in those big brown eyes
Filled with tears she tried to hide . . . she said . . .
Oh . . . oh oh oh . . . it's my first time
Oh . . . oh oh oh . . . please be kind
Oh . . . oh oh oh . . . don't hurt me

When he pulled out blood dribbled onto his car seat. He was like, "Don't worry about that." He didn't ask if it was my first time so I didn't say so. He flung the condom out of the window. That second, a cop knocked on the glass. *What the fuck.* He shined a flashlight inside the car, on me. I was naked. I covered my body with my hands. He was like, "What are you kids up to?" Jake was like, "Nothing, sir." The cop hovered the light over Jake's eyes. "Littering is a crime, son. Get out, pick that up, and throw it in the bin."

Jake got out, with just his boxers on, to retrieve the rubber. Meanwhile, the cop shone the light on my body. He was like, "Are you all right in there, miss?"

When Jake came back to the car the cop lectured him, mentioning "warnings" and "three strikes" and stuff. Then he left us alone. It's a miracle I didn't faint in the meantime. I got dressed as Jake drove me home.

"That was fucked-up," I said. "He shined his light all over me. Is it shined or shone? Anyway, where did he come from? Was he parked behind us the whole time? Watching us? What a pervert. I feel so degraded."

"Listen, Kat, the condom broke."

"What?"

"When I picked it up, I saw it was broken."

"Maybe it broke when you threw it? The pavement tore it?"

"Don't know . . . you aren't on the pill?"

"No."

"We gotta get you Plan B."

"How? I can't tell my mom."

"I have a pharmacy hookup."

"Yeah, I can see that."

When I got home, Mom was on the couch watching *The Sopranos*. She asked how my night with Lucy was. I ran upstairs.

THE WOODS

Getting up for Weaver Street was easy, since I couldn't fall asleep in the first place. Mom and I were silent in the car. She got pancakes and read the newspaper. I got coffee and stared blankly into the back of Mom's newspaper. Jake texted me, "got your pill." I told him to meet me in the parking lot. From the car window he handed me a paper bag. He was stern, father-like, when he said take it immediately. He also said it's normal to feel sick afterward. I was like how do you know so much about Plan B? He shook his head, don't ask. I took the pill in the bathroom of Weaver Street. The directions on the box said I'd have to take another pill in a few hours, so I shoved that one in my pocket. I came back to Mom like, sorry I took forever, I had to poop. She was like, I didn't need to know that. The rest of the day was ridden with stomach cramps. I felt miserable. I felt like a woman. A sexually active woman who knew things she shouldn't. Who understood the world. I stared outside my window all day, unable to study, play piano, read comics, cut clothes, pluck my eyebrows, eat grilled cheese, or watch TV. I looked for the deer but they didn't come. I wondered if animals could sense that I wasn't a virgin. Did my mom see it on my face? I couldn't see a difference in the mirror, though I searched for it. My eyes were still round and hooded. My face still plump with baby fat. Or collagen, they call it in the fashion magazines. My eyebrows were still thin and arched, stuck in a state of surprise. My face didn't demonstrate any progress or unrest. But inside something shattered. It wasn't all bad. I felt liberated. I fell asleep on a pile of clothes and dreamed of Dexter running with deer. I chased him deep into the woods but he ran too fast. My feet were stuck in the mud. I was trapped. My head hurt. I rubbed my scalp to find stumps, two horns growing.

THE NIGHTLIGHT

I heard the school bell ring from off campus more often than inside a classroom. I was a renegade. Ashley was my best friend, Charlie was a stranger, and Nosebleed was like a brother, in that we were close but not *chummy*. There was a barrier between us, a warning: intimacy may lead to incest. Madeline went to rehab for cutting. Who knew. I was barely scraping by with my grades. As and Bs became Cs and Ds. I'd hand in blank quizzes. Just write my name and take a nap. On a standardized test once I penciled in:

a
  c
a
  b
a
  c
a

b
a
c
a
b
a
c
a
b
a
c
a
b
a
c
a
b

ACAB.

My math teacher took me aside one day and warned that if I "keep this up" I won't graduate. I was like, who says I wanna graduate? He got all flustered, like, I don't know what's going on with you, but it isn't worth ruining your future, blah, blah, blah. I explained to him that every future is ruined, we all end up in the ground, with or without a diploma. He ignored that and added, don't you know education means independence? What a dummy. There's no such thing as independence in this world. The system is rigged. It sets you up for selling your soul and if you refuse to do that, you're a failure. There's no middle ground. If you play along, you get a rotten deal. The only ones who really know how to live are out on the streets. That's real freedom. He was like, that's a lot of mumbo-jumbo just to avoid studying. I told him he doesn't understand anarchy.

"Grow up," he said.

"I'd rather die."

Piano was moving along without passion. Even Chopin couldn't arouse me. My teacher hated me. He got livid at each crescendo I ignored, any time signature I overlooked. I drowned everything in a sustain pedal, even staccato. I played *piano* as *forte* and vice versa. He put me on a metronome, for fuck's sake. When I asked him for the recommendation letter he said, "I thought you gave up on that." What gave you that impression? I asked. He was like, "You're rebelling against your music." Before he praised my "interpretations" and now they were "erratic"? Typical. To tell the truth I couldn't recall why I wanted to go away so badly. Being in high school didn't suck too much now that I skipped all my classes.

Jake settled into his place. His dad gave him a mattress, which he put on the floor.

He got a rug from a friend, a table from the thrift shop, and a plastic shelf off the street, for the television. He said he spent tons of money on the TV and DVD player. A paper bag full of cash from Driade, no doubt. He stacked books and CDs on the floor and had a minifridge full of forties. Scratched skateboards lounged in various corners. Clothes were folded in trash bags. Christmas lights and candles served as decoration and his only light source. A space heater burned red and smelled like something from childhood I couldn't put my finger on.

We had sex all the time, even on school days. If I hung around Driade, he'd take me to the shed on his lunch break. If I was at school, he'd pick me up from there. It didn't hurt anymore. The pain in the ass was after the fact. Once he came I had to run to the main house, through the lawn, often barefoot and half-naked, to use the bathroom. It was annoying, so I avoided using the bathroom for as long as I could. So I got UTIs. And Jake hooked me up with pharmaceuticals.

Sundays after Weaver Street Mom would drop me off at the main house (where she thought Jake lived). When she drove away, I'd scuttle to the shed. Sunday was a school night, typically off-limits for socializing. But she made an exception because he was my "boyfriend" and because I complained about not being free, like my friends. "Lucy goes out all weekend. She goes to crazy house parties and comes home drunk in the morning. I'm the only dummy with a curfew who can't go out on school nights." I didn't know if Lucy actually did any of that, but the argument convinced Mom. She didn't know about my skipping, lifting, or lying, of course.

Sunday was Jake's day off and I was allowed to stay with him from noon to nine.

He insisted I come over every Sunday, even though he never stayed awake for it. I'd knock on his door and he'd open up after five minutes, sleepy and grumpy. He'd grumble hello and turn around and hop back into bed. He'd sleep for hours, while I read, watched movies, or slept next to him. Mostly I just stared at the back of his neck. He slept peacefully. When he woke up he'd say, "I was dreaming about you. You're my dream girl." He'd hug me, kiss me, smother me in affection, and we'd have sex and then he'd go back to sleep. And I'd cross the lawn.

The sleep was a baffling addition to our relationship. I didn't expect it or welcome it. At the beginning I'd try to wake him up and ask him to take me out. It irritated him. He'd be like, "Let's just be together." I resigned. I'd rather watch Jake sleep than do anything else on a Sunday. I told myself that spending all day in bed together was mature. We didn't need dates. We didn't need distractions. We didn't even need to talk.

We were in love.

Valentine's Day came and went. Jake said he didn't celebrate "that shit." I had spent several days laboring over a painting of two aliens sitting on the rings of a planet, tentacles tangled into a heart . . . when I gave it to him he said it made him feel guilty. That night he told me he loved me. Well, he began to. We were sitting in his car and the windows were foggy because it was warm inside and freezing outside.

He started writing, with his finger, on the glass of his window: I-L-O-V-E-Y-O

He stopped there and turned to look at me. I was like, "I love you."

He turned back and finished writing: G-U-R-T

"I love yogurt," he said. Tears welled up in my eyes.

He was like, "Kat. Of course I love you. I was kidding."

Bob was my enemy. After our disastrous date I stopped going to his shop. So he started coming to mine. He tried acting normal toward me, as if nothing happened. I was cold in return. I shunned him, like I didn't know him. So he turned vile. He creeped around my store during his bathroom breaks, smoke breaks (he didn't smoke), *and* lunch breaks. Once he brought a sandwich in with him and ate it while terrorizing me. When I told him to *fuck off* or that I was *calling the cops* it only made him nastier. I wouldn't talk *with* him but he'd talk *to* me. Dirty stuff, what he would have "done to me" had I stayed at his, or if he could "have me" again.

"I'll go down on you for hours, get you in the mood . . . I'll get a hotel suite for a weekend and lock you in . . . You'll beg me for more . . . I could have made you come ten times."

It was bizarre and uncomfortable. I was always alone in the store, so I couldn't rely on customers or colleagues to bail me out. He didn't scare me, but he made me feel gross. In retrospect, my crush on him had been juvenile. He never deserved it. What drew me to him in the first place was bewildering. I guess it was the comics. How I missed Chapel Hill Comics. I hadn't bought a new comic in weeks. Magazines became my new life source. Even online magazines, like *Gunshot*. I kept up with everything Sabrina Mink posted. Sometimes I considered reaching out to her. "Remember me? Bitch?"

One night, I saw Bob at Time-Out with a chubby girl. The one who asked him out, no doubt. She looked sweet. I felt bad for her. Soon I'd finish my community service hours. Before all this happened, I'd hoped to stay at the bookstore, as paid staff.

I'd even learn to use the register. But with Bob around . . . I couldn't fathom it.

March Madness arrived. The streets were packed with UNC fans. They were going nuts. We either won or lost, I couldn't tell, the reaction was crazy regardless. I took Jake to the Nightlight. During the day it was the Skylight, a café and bookstore. At night it turned into a mini-nightclub for dance parties and shows. Andrew was playing that night. We were friends in middle school. He wasn't one of the skaters who molested me or one of the druggies who got me pills. He was always around trouble but not in it. We lost touch since he went to Chapel Hill High, not East, and never came to Dexter's. He told me once that he cared too much about "his craft" (music) to get wasted. He was punk rock on the outside but on the inside he was wholesome. One night he called my home number. I saw his name on the caller ID and thought, *What does he want from me?* I let it go to voice mail. He left a message inviting me to his gig. Good excuse to take Jake out of the shed.

Andrew got tall and good-looking. Even his braces suited him. His hair was ironed over his face, his pants were too tight (even for punk standards), his shirt was bright flannel, and his wrists were stacked with bracelets. "Shit," I said when I hugged him. "You're emo." I introduced him to Jake, who was rude, for no reason. Jake was only nice to me.

Andrew had a one-man band called Buckthorne Superstar. Before his set he said into the mic, "This first song is dedicated to my friend Kat." He pointed to me and everyone looked. "It's called 'Groupie Superstar.' "

Jake looked at me like, *What?* And I looked back at him like, *I dunno.* The song was fast and good and the lyrics were incomprehensible. Thank God. Jake avoided the internet like the plague—he didn't have a laptop and his shed didn't have Wi-Fi. I never worried about him finding the article online. In person, Jake hated gossip and small talk. So he probably wouldn't hear my story from our friends. Plus, now that I was officially His Girl, nobody would dare bring me up to him, unless they wanted to say something nice. Punk boys made the best boyfriends because they were possessive and scary. Of course *I'd* be the one to drag us into a potential trap.

The rest of the set went by in a nervous blur for me and boredom for him. After the show everyone stood in the alley outside the venue. I sent Jake to get a forty from a crackhead. Andrew and I were alone for a minute. He asked if I liked the song.

"I can't believe you wrote a song for me. It's sick."

"I had to, before Trippy does."

"Haha." I tried to change the subject. "Great gig, dude. I'm impressed."

It didn't work. He was beyond excited, stuck on it. "You're the impressive one.

What's Trippy like? Do y'all talk?"

Jake approached with the paper bag and I gave Andrew a look, like, *Shut the fuck up, please.* He took the hint. He was always a smart kid. The next thing he said really loud, so Jake would hear we were talking about "normal" stuff.

"So. How's Lucy?"

"I wouldn't know. We don't talk anymore." I took a swig of the forty and offered it to Andrew. He declined.

"No way. I loved Lucy. What happened to her?"

"She's not dead. We just don't talk."

"Ah, damn." Pause. "How's East? How's piano?"

"I ditch school a lot. Piano's fine, but . . . I'm uninspired."

Andrew was bummed out by my life. "That sucks," he said.

Jake pointed across the alley and said, "Those chicks look demented." He hyena-laughed. They charged toward us like ghouls, in striped shirts with boat collars and microminis with wide belts. They wore slip-on checkered Vans, ridiculous leggings, and tortured hairdos that resembled tumbleweeds. Their makeup was clownish, like they did it in the dark. Emo girls made punk girls look bad, because normies, preps, townies, and squares confused us for each other. Which made no sense. We couldn't be more different. They listened to Fall Out Boy, My Chemical Romance, and AFI. No self-respect. The emo chicks came up to Andrew and fawned all over him. I cringed visibly. Andrew was like, "Gotta go. Nice seeing you, Kat." As I watched Andrew walk away, a brick of nostalgia hit me in the face. What I longed for, I couldn't say.

"That's the last time we go to an emo show," Jake said.

"I thought it would be fun."

"It wasn't. Wanna go home? Or to Dexter's?"

He never took me to Dexter's. It started out as a reaction to Dexter's overdose, but over a month had passed. And I only hung out with Jake. Ashley, when we lifted. Nosebleed, in his car. I never went out alone anymore. Andrew's show was my first *concert* since Trippy Dope.

Huh. I considered the shed, stomping barefoot on mud to tiptoe over grimy floors to hover over a filthy toilet. "Let's go to Dexter's."

In the car I couldn't sit still. I was ecstatic in the face of fun. I couldn't wait to see Dexter. Ashley told me he recovered, in terms of not overdosing again. But he was still using, like everyone else. When did they get into heroin? I wondered if that's why Jake slept so much. Was he that tired? Or "nodding out," a term I learned in the Miles Davis book my piano teacher lent me. I didn't care. I was going back to the Lab.

The Casualties play live in the Party Room. Ashley and Dexter are dressed in Renaissance frocks, powdered wigs on their heads and hearts on their cheeks. They're dancing arm in arm. Charlie's playing cards. He's in a tuxedo, stunning, cigar hanging from his mouth. Yes, I'm ready to be friends again. No, no hard feelings. I missed you too. I missed you more than you missed me. Nosebleed lets his mohawk down. He made something for us, in the kitchen. A pyramid of champagne glasses towering up to the ceiling, with malt liquor cascading out of them, onto the floor. This is it, guys. The greatest night of our lives.

THE BACK PORCH

"Bummer," I said to Jake.

"It's always a bummer."

"*You* came late to the party." I yawned. "It used to be fun."

Jake and I showed up at Dexter's without texting anyone. We wanted to surprise them, we thought they'd be bouncing off the walls. Nobody noticed us come in. We went straight to the kitchen for beer. Muffled music seeped out of the Party Room, I couldn't make out the band but it sounded like squatter punk. Not Dexter's taste. The voices behind the fridge door were hushed. I couldn't see anyone except some kid, passed out facedown in the hallway. "Who's that?" I asked Jake. "Beats me," he said. The kid's body shot up and I recognized Little Tim. He was playing his "punk's dead" prank. He ran up behind me, put me in a headlock, and punched me in the stomach. "I got you," he shouted.

"Ow, Tim." I pushed him off and rubbed my belly.

"Watch me fight these hoppers." Little Tim punched the air. He had natural amphetamines pumping through his veins.

"Who?"

"Train hoppers hogging the Party Room."

I gawked at Jake and he shrugged at me. Tim continued.

"They're from Mississippi. Trying to score. They smell like dogshit."

"Mississippi?" I asked, wide-eyed.

"Uh, yeah, Kat, it's a state? In the United States of America?" He used that voice little kids use when making fun of "retarded" people. Little Tim was nearly thirteen now, too old to do that. I didn't feel like lecturing him. Anyway, before I could, he ran off to the bathroom. To jizz on a wall or kick a door or smash a mirror into pieces.

"Did you hear that?" I said to Jake. "Hoppers from Mississippi. Let's meet them." I was frantic, feverish, on the verge of collapse. *Could it be? Was he here? My Josh?* I failed to consider that Jake would be there to witness it, our reunion, what I've dreamed of for months.

"Sounds stinky," Jake said. "Can we go home? Nobody knows we're here. They won't know we left."

"No way. I'm sick of the shed."

"You're sick of the love shack?" He was wounded.

"I love it, Jake. It's *wonderful.*" The irony in my voice was harsh. "But let me have tonight?" Not waiting for his answer, I walked ahead of him and charged into the Party Room. Who was this brazen girl standing up to her boyfriend? Was her power sourced from the idea of seeing her long-lost love? Or was she just sick of holding in pee?

I barged in like a woman on a mission. I scanned the room for faces. Nodded at Dexter, smiled at Charlie (he didn't smile back), winked at Ashley, and blew a kiss to Nosebleed. The new faces were dirty, looked like they had dried mud on them. Dreads, floppy mohawks, mullets, rattails, bandanas, clothes that were once white now brown . . . faces, faces, faces, bright blue eyes, black hair with blond roots, a ski slope nose, full lips, long limbs, Misfits T-shirt with holes in it, held together with safety pins, basically a rag . . . *Josh.*

My Josh. I shivered at the sight of him. He was stunning, though he lost too much weight. Jake was like, "Kat, breathe. It stinks but you'll get used to it." I hadn't realized I stopped breathing. It wasn't for the reason he thought. I exhaled. Jake didn't know about Josh. There was nothing to know, we never "did" anything, we were "just friends." It takes two people to be in a relationship but only one to be in love. It takes two people to make a relationship but only one to end it.

Jake went over to our crew. I stayed put, staring at Josh. A buddy of his nudged him and pointed at me, like, *She's checking you out, dude.* Josh met my eyes and smiled so big it burst me.

He waved coyly. "Come here, Kat." Everyone could hear because everyone was whispering for some reason. Jake and Charlie watched me walk over to him and sit down. They looked at me, like, *What are you doing?* Screw them both. Josh did stink but I didn't mind. His scent was yummy, like Dexter's. My little skunk.

Josh hugged me hard and I squeezed back harder. I could feel all the bones in his back. Like hugging a seashell. We pulled away and stared at each other for a moment, then we both tried talking at the same time:

"I WHERE wanted DID to YOU call GO you??"

We laughed at that then I let him talk first.

"I was gonna call but we just got here. Had to touch base, find a phone. You look good. I dig the hair."

"Thanks. You too. That's okay. Where have you been?"

"All around, mostly Mississippi. We hopped trains, dumpster-dived, stole, and slept under bridges. It was great. I learned to play the banjo."

"Wow," I said. "Did you . . . find Sarah?"

"Sarah . . . was pregnant when I got there."

"Oh, shit." *She was pregnant? Hahaha bitch. What a dumb bitch. Fuck you, Sarah, I win I win I win!* "I'm sorry."

"It's all right. When I saw her I realized I wasn't really in love with her. We're more like brother and sister."

"I get it. I've got something like that with Nosebleed."

I motioned over at Nosebleed, who was trying to spit into a cup on the floor. After a couple of tries, he got it and said, "Did y'all see that?"

Josh leered. "Since when?"

"Lots changed since you left. Like, *lots*."

"Tell me."

"You sticking around?"

"Let's smoke outside."

"We can smoke inside." I glanced at Jake, who was watching me.

"I prefer the back porch," Josh said, getting up, scattering dust around him like Pig-Pen, then pulling me up with his hands.

"I'm going for a smoke," I said to Jake.

"Y'all can smoke in here," Dexter said.

"We know," said Josh. "Come on, Kat."

Ooh, the looks we got.

The back porch wasn't used much. Smoking inside was a luxury most of us could only dream of, since most of us lived with our parents. The ones without parents didn't have an "inside" at all. Another reason nobody used the porch was because it was a dump. Piles of trash, random gadgets, and motor parts collected rust. The third reason nobody used the porch was because North Carolina was either too hot or too cold for us, with our limited outfit range. Punks were only comfortable in September and April. Josh shivered in his raggy shirt. I offered him my jacket and he declined. We sat on a soggy cardboard box. I hoped my body provided some heat.

"What's the deal in there?" I asked Josh.

"I was gonna ask you. Ain't that your crew?"

"Oh, the boys are just being dicks. That's not what I meant. Why's everyone acting sketchy? It's usually a different vibe."

"Well, my friends are trying to score. Your friends have a connect, we're negotiating, bartering, you know the deal."

"I see. Are you into all that?"

"Nah." He shook his head. "You?"

"No. I don't know where it came from. I haven't really been present."

"Where have you been?"

I paused, considered my odds, and went for it. "Can you keep a secret?"

"Of course."

"I can't believe I'm telling you this. I haven't told anybody."

"Give it to me."

"There's this rumor about me and Trippy Dope."

"Trippy Dope? The rock star? What rumor?"

"This journalist ran a story, with a picture of me and Trippy, saying I'm a groupie and I got with him after his show at Cat's Cradle."

"Trip played the Cradle? Dammit."

"Yeah, you were gone. Anyway, the story got out and everyone, I mean *everyone* saw it. And now it's too late to tell the truth."

"It's never too late to tell the truth."

"Josh, you don't get it. The news spread like wildfire. And I mean, it wasn't all bad. My reputation soared, I got some perks. But keeping up with appearances? It's hard to explain, but, because of that story, one thing led to another, and now everything changed."

"How so?"

"First off, I have this boyfriend."

"The one you came in with?"

"Yeah. Jake is cool, but, my life has spiraled."

"Spiraled, Kat? You're talkin' to a homeless kid."

"Obviously mine are 'middle-class' problems. But you know who I am, you know what my parents are like. I'm failing school, I suck at piano."

"You don't suck at piano. And I didn't see the article. Does that help?"

"Because you don't have a computer. Actually, my boyfriend hasn't seen it, either. It's kind of why he's my boyfriend."

"I see."

"It's hard to explain. After you left, everything got messed up. So what I'm trying to say is . . . I blame you." I laughed. Talking to Josh was easy.

"Hah. That's fair. I disappeared. But I didn't say bye because I knew I'd come back. Plus, you told me . . . how you felt and it freaked me out."

"Yeah, I know. Sorry."

"Don't be sorry. I love you too, I told you."

"But not *like that*, you said."

"Well, I thought I had Sarah, I didn't know what I wanted. Now I know."

"Know what?"

"I want to be with you."

"What?" I croaked.

"I want us sleeping under the stars. Life's too short not to. I'll teach you about the street. Dumpster-diving. Panhandling. Robbing. You can play the harmonica to my banjo. We can start a band. There's an incredible community out there, you wouldn't believe it. You'll feel at home, everywhere."

Josh looked so blissful while recounting the wonderful skills he wanted to share with me. He really meant what he was promising. I realized how silly I was to share my suburban problems with him. He didn't have a school to flunk out of, or parents to disappoint. He didn't have a reputation to keep up. I wanted to be like him. I wanted to be free. I was blown away by what he was offering. I kissed him, fast, and pulled away.

"I can't believe I did that, my boyfriend's inside."

"Screw him." He kissed me back.

The biggest rush of my life was interrupted by footsteps.

"Someone's coming," I whimpered. We pulled away.

Jake jumped outside with Charlie. He was like, "What's up?"

"Nothing. Smoking."

"You're done?" Jake asked me.

"Oh, we didn't light up yet. Do you have a cigarette, Josh?"

"I thought you had a cigarette," Josh said to me. We looked at each other, like, *Oops*.

I turned back to Jake and asked him for a cigarette. Jake handed me one from his pack. I was like, "Can Josh have one, too?" Jake passed Josh a cigarette.

Josh and I sat and smoked while Charlie and Jake stood and smoked behind us. Nobody spoke. Weirdest cigarette break ever. When we finished, the boys flicked their butts into the yard and I put mine out with my shoe (I never learned how to flick butts). We went back inside, Jake grabbing my hand.

Back in the Party Room, everyone was placated and satiated. They sat like children at story time. Cross-legged, leaning on each other, some lying down. A cloud of calm. Ashley had her head on Dexter's shoulders and Dexter's eyes were closed.

Only Little Tim and Nosebleed were drinking forties, talking loud and looking for trouble.

I said to Josh, "Talk later?" He was like, "You bet," and he went to his crusty friends while I went to mine. Jake was like, "I'm taking a leak," so I sat down with Charlie. He looked me in the face. Did that mean he was open to talking? I seized the opportunity. Maybe it would go well . . . being honest with Josh did wonders. A night of miracles.

"Hey, Charlie? Can we talk?"

"We are talking."

"I'm sorry about everything."

"Forget it, Kit Kat." I forgot he called me that. "How's life with Jake?"

"It's good."

"Jake's my boy."

"Y'all are close?"

"He's here all the time."

"Really?"

"Yeah, he's our man."

Our man . . . what did that remind me of? The Velvet Underground song. "Can I ask you something?"

"Shoot."

"When did everyone go hard-core?"

"In what way?"

I looked around and lowered my voice. "Where's the . . . *junk* coming from?"

Charlie looked at me like I was nuts. "Kit Kat, you serious?" He looked around and lowered his voice. "Jake is *the man*."

"Charlie . . . stop."

"He's our guy, our supply. He's got the Mexican connection."

"Since when?"

"Uh . . . since when you met him? The big party night."

"But . . . he's never here."

"He's never here *with you.*"

"I don't believe this," I said.

"You don't have to. Anyway, no hard feelings. I can see your type is skeezy rocker or sleazy dealer." With that, he got up and walked off. He burned me and I deserved it. I was dumb to think he wanted to be friends. What Charlie told me was too much to process so I pushed it away. I had a briefcase stuffed full of feelings that I kept locked and shoved under the bed in my brain.

Keeping it together that evening was easy, at that point I was good at pretending.

Jake and I had a few beers with the crew, who were barely interactive. Was everyone high? Was Jake? I barely cared. Josh and I made eyes the whole time. Before Jake drove me home I made Josh promise he'd call me. He recited my number by memory.

THE CAVE

"I can't stop thinking about you," Josh said on the phone the next day.

"Me too," I gushed.

"So . . . about what I said last night."

"Yeah?"

"What do you think?"

"What did you say last night?" I knew what he said, I played it in my head a hundred times. But I wanted to hear him say it.

"Running away with me."

"Oh, yeah, that." My whole body shook.

"You down?"

"I'm down." I was going to faint.

"Meet me at the Cave, Tuesday night," he instructed.

"I can't go out on school nights, remember?"

"There's a show. I know your mom makes exceptions for shows. Anyway, you're running away. Just sneak out a window."

"Breaking the rules is easier under the pretense of following rules."

"Whatever floats your boat. Just be there."

The plan was crazy but I felt crazy. Nothing grounded me. I loved Jake, but I didn't know him. Charlie hated me more than I thought. My friends weren't available to me in any profound way. Ashley and Nosebleed would never let me in. I was approaching dropout status at school. Running away was the only way to avoid confronting my parents about my report card, arriving by mail any day.

What do you pack for running away, without being too obvious? I stuffed my backpack full of underwear, socks, and comfy "road" clothes. No makeup, just soap, tampons, tweezers, Old Spice, and sunscreen. A copy of *Catcher in the Rye*, my favorite CDs, and a Walkman. Granola bars and my cell phone. My parents paid my phone bill. I considered the absurdity but it didn't hit me. I took an extra-long shower, to make up for potential weeks (months?) of not showering. (Years?)

I read somewhere, probably in *Teen Vogue*, that most adolescents who survive suicide attempts are relieved. They admit they didn't consider the reality of dying, truly, as in, *no way back*. Their suicide fantasies involved interacting with their friends afterward, witnessing people's reactions at their funeral, getting redemption or revenge. The whole point of their suicide was to attain a reaction in the world they were leaving. Adolescent brains are developing, so these concepts can seem muddy, out of reach. Up for interpretation. Poetry.

Similar thoughts rushed through me as I got ready that evening. I saw running away from everything as the only way to fix anything. I wasn't *abandoning* my family, friends, and school . . . I was *improving* my bond to those people, *fulfilling* my responsibilities, by vanishing. If I removed myself from something, I couldn't fuck it up. Does that make sense? Not to anyone who hasn't felt it. Anyway, it didn't matter what I had in my head. I had a backpack full of supplies and two hoodies under my jacket.

Mom dropped me off and I got emotional saying bye. I hugged her for too long and told her too earnestly that I loved her. Before I lost my cool I ran out and didn't look back. Teardrops dotted the steps leading to the Cave, a basement music venue. It was cool as hell, but rarely hosted all-ages shows, like the one I descended into. I didn't know the band, it was bluegrass. Josh picked whatever would let us in. I ordered a Diet Coke and took a seat at the bar. As I watched the crowd trickle in I immersed myself in the romance of my decision.

Nobody here can imagine what you're about to do. Nobody here has felt the love that you do. Your boyfriend is just blocks away, in his shed. Or a couple of streets down, dealing out heroin. Meanwhile, his girlfriend—YOU—sit perched on a stool, in secret, sipping cola. You're waiting for someone else. Your homeless god, your runaway prince, your out-of-work supermodel, his soul too potent to capture in a portrait.

"Miss, someone sitting there?" A hillbilly with a beer belly poked me on the shoulder, then pointed to the stool I set my backpack on.

"He's coming." I grinned.

He frowned and shifted his weight between his feet. I thought, *Sir, if only you knew the importance of the seat I withheld from you. If only you understood the value of what's inside this backpack.*

After half an hour the hillbilly shot me a look, like, *Is that seat still saved?* Yes, I replied with my eyes. *He's a little late. He's got no car, no cash for bus fare. He'll find a way, he always does, he's a genius. Pure of heart and full of brain. Give him time, he'll prove it, you'll see why I wouldn't let you sit here.*

I ordered another Coke, this one regular, full sugar.

The bluegrass band was killer. They had grit. Their crowd was rustic and rowdy. I memorized them all, since I spent two hours searching the space for his face. I had no way to reach him. My phone hadn't buzzed. I drank three Cokes and didn't go to the bathroom, in fear of his coming down and not being able to find me. *Coming down coming down coming down DOWN.* Shit, I was in a basement. Maybe I had no reception? I ran out and upstairs, to the street. Full signal, no missed calls. No texts, no sign of Josh. Just my backpack and me.

I peed in a bush and waited on the street for an hour.

Come get your roadkill. I read my book under a streetlamp and watched the Cave crowd pour out of the venue and pair off. Some rolled into their cars and others walked down Franklin, to the bars.

I opened my phone to one text, from Mom. "It's getting late." In another dimension, I was arm in arm with Josh, on a train or lying in the back of a pickup truck.

I'd get the text from Mom and feel far away from her. Maybe I'd cry. Josh would console me. *Being wild is impossible if you aren't free. Being free is pointless if you aren't wild.* But I wasn't in that dimension of space and time. I was in the one where I ended up alone and heartbroken on Franklin Street.

"Come get me."

In the car I was *this close* to confessing everything and asking for help. *Mom, I'm desperate. I need a shrink, a week on Topsail Island, a dozen grilled cheese sandwiches and Adult Swim on 24/7. I need shock therapy and a lobotomy. A crisp white hospital gown with the butt out. An empty head and a new reality.* But I said nothing because I didn't want to ruin the tragic relief of being in the car with Mom. I just turned up the radio, 89.3.

In bed I laughed at myself. Tears soaked my pillow. *You were really gonna go there, huh?* I was afraid of myself. Under the covers I clung to the Care Bear.

The dog slept outside my door.

THE LOVE SHACK

Josh was too ashamed to confront me. Or he got hit by a bus, but I didn't hope for that. I wasn't angry with him. His silence was gracious. Ditching a girl on a date is one thing, but convincing her to pack her whole life (or what's left of it) into a backpack and *then* ditching her? Unforgivable. But I was over it. A cigarette lit backwards. Josh didn't show because he knew I couldn't leave with him, not really. My mind would have changed the minute I saw him. I swear. I belonged to Jake. I carried the love shack in my heart.

Ashley was a true friend, after all. She helped me forge a fake report card for my parents, using an old one I kept. Previous Kat's grades. How did old Kat do it? New Kat did not know. I intercepted the current card the school sent, since I always got home first. Opening the envelope wasn't necessary, I knew the catastrophe it contained. I tore it, tossed it in the trash, threw the trash into the dumpster, considered lighting the dumpster on fire but didn't have a lighter. The school started sending letters concerning my absences, too. Those were piling up. The first month of skipping was fine. The teachers believed my forged sick notes, since I'd always been "good." It's crazy what you can get away with when people trust you. That trust was running thin and I had to tread carefully or I'd break through the ice and fall into a freezing abyss: after-school detention.

"Let's go to Driade?" I asked Jake one Sunday. We were lying in bed, watching *The Royal Tenenbaums* for the millionth time. We spent hours at Visart Video every weekend just to end up renting the same thing. Jake was more alert than usual, so I thought we could go for a coffee.

"Forget Driade." He sighed. "I got laid off."

"What? Why?"

"They accused me of stealing. Can you believe it?"

"Well . . . you do steal."

"What?"

"Babe, I see you taking money from the register."

He wouldn't look at me, his eyes stayed glued on Gwyneth Paltrow.

"Jake." I got in his face. "I don't care that you steal. But I'm curious. Where do you spend it all? You've got the stolen cash *plus* your paycheck *plus* tips *plus* . . . drug money?" He looked at me like a stunned deer. I went on before he could interrupt. "Your rent is what? Two hundred bucks? You never take me out. You don't go shopping. Are you saving up for a yacht?"

"You never ask me to take you out."

"God, Jake, that's not the point. And not true. A whole different argument."

"All right."

"All right? So?"

"So, what?"

"So where do you spend all your money?."

"I . . . owe some people . . . some money."

"Oh, great." I fell back onto my pillow dramatically.

"That's why I sell drugs. I wouldn't do it otherwise."

"Sure." I channeled Carmela Soprano. "You're a saint."

"How do you know about that anyway?"

"Charlie told me."

He punched his pillow. "I was so careful, to protect you. Fuck Charlie." He rolled around, turning his back to me.

"It's not *his* fault. You should be honest with me. I'm your girlfriend."

"*You're* one to talk," he snapped.

"What's that mean?"

"Oh, I think you know."

"I have no idea."

"Should I ask Trippy Dope?"

Thanks to Josh, that was nothing. I was relieved he didn't say, "What about that crusty boy you kissed the other night? What about the hillbilly spy I hired to check on you at the Cave? What about your plan to break my heart, abandon me, and never look back?" So, Trippy Dope? Piece of cake.

"Yeah, what *about* Trippy Dope? You read the article? So did everyone else, congratulations," I huffed.

"Yeah but unlike everyone else, *I know* that it's bullshit, Kat. *I* took your virginity. You bled all over my car."

"Virginity is a social construct."

"Oh, God. Here we go." He stood up abruptly and started pulling his pants on.

Leave it to a boy to turn a conversation about *him* stealing money and dealing drugs . . . into a conversation about a girl's virginity? He was being a dickhead. Still I felt sympathy and tenderness toward him . . . he was so stupid, trying to pull his jeans on, to rebel against me, as if I were his mom. I wanted to let him win.

"I didn't tell you because I wanted you to like me. I didn't want you to judge me, like everyone else. I didn't want you to expect things from me."

He paused and let the pants drop to his feet. "I'm glad it's bullshit. Trippy Dope's a hack." He stood there, back turned to me, pants in a puddle, waiting to be invited back to bed. Too stubborn to do it himself.

"Come back to bed."

He came back to bed.

That was our first fight. We celebrated it with passionate lovemaking. Then I petted his hair as he slept next to me. I fell immensely in love. I thought I already loved him before that moment, and I did, with my head. But that day my soul connected to his, irreversibly. My spirit.

Jake is part of you. Your body is a vessel for his love. You will only think of Jake.

There is nobody else. You could live purely off his touch. You lack nothing. You never need to go out again. You could live your life in this shed. Why would you go anywhere else? Just kissing him is more thrilling than slam-dancing with skinheads. And more dangerous. He's your family. Your future. Your life.

I completed my community service sentence. I'd never have to see Bob again. I'd miss the bookstore. Mom was elated. She was like, let's go out and celebrate. We went to Elmo's Diner, during brunch. The line was out the door. Elmo's gave out free coffee for people waiting for a spot. Our names weren't called even after we finished our mugs.

Mom didn't like waiting in line. My guess was lines reminded her of communism. So we went to Weaver Street.

No community service meant I could practice piano all day on Saturday. I crammed for my audition. My teacher finally wrote the recommendation letter. It was sealed when he handed it to me, but I imagined he wrote something immensely flattering. I packed the letter into the folder of materials I'd present at the audition, including my (old) school grades and an essay I wrote on the *Minute Waltz* being a punk rock masterpiece. I was getting in for sure. Jake and I discussed it and he said that when he paid people off he could move to Winston-Salem to be close to me. Every town had coffee shops and junkies, right?

"Kat, can I ask you a favor?"

"Anything." I kissed Jake on the neck. My new favorite part of his body. I chose a favorite spot to worship every time I saw him. He brushed me away.

"Come on, that tickles. Listen. I'm having a hard time without Driade. I'll find a new job but till then I need a hand. You wanna help?"

"Of course."

Jake led me to Maron's room. It looked and smelled like a head shop. There was an iguana in a cage I tried not to look at because it made me sad. I wondered if Maron ever let the guy out in the yard. Or let him walk around the house. I wondered if I could offer to babysit him. Or offer to take him home. He could live with me in my room. "Kat, stop looking at the iguana." Jake hated when I didn't pay attention to him. I made a mental note to think about the iguana later, when I had more time, and work out an escape plan.

Jake took a plastic shopping bag out of Maron's closet and set it on the bed. Inside of that bag was a brown paper bag. From the brown bag he pulled a big brown lump wrapped in clear plastic. Another bag was pulled out of the brown paper bag, which held tiny deflated balloons.

"You're like Mary Poppins with this magic bag." I tried sounding normal but I was freaking out. I thought, *Why is he exposing you to this? Why couldn't he keep it for himself and let you pretend it's not happening?*

"What is all this?" I stuttered.

"Kat, you're either down or not. I'm not gonna baby you."

"Okay. Tell me what to do." I stiffened.

"So here's the big daddy lump." He patted the block of heroin. "I have to measure out little baby lumps. *Your* job is to wrap the baby lumps up in balloons. Like pigs in a blanket."

I nodded like it was school. The way he explained it was touching. If you really thought about it, what I was handling could have been anything. Heroin was just atoms and particles like anything else was. It was a plant. A naturally occurring phenomenon. How was it so different from an apple or from my face? I enjoyed busywork, tasks involving my hands. Wrapping and snapping the rubber around the packed brown lumps. It was meditative, like piano. Of course some negative thoughts tried to penetrate, asking what the hell I was doing. When that happened I simply considered my loyalty, my purpose.

You're devoted to Jake. He's the only one here for you. He knows everything and still loves you. The faster he pays his due, the sooner he can stop. You aren't dealing, you're just on an assembly line. The junkies who buy it buy it anyway, regardless of who ties the baggies. May as well be you.

"You've got such delicate fingers," Jake said, admiring.

"Do you do this stuff?" I asked.

"It's not a big deal. I don't shoot up."

"You smoke it?"

"Nah."

"Snort it?"

"Not how you think. It's not a powder, as you see. I developed a method."

He opened up a drawer from the cabinet the iguana was on. He pulled out a rolled-up shirt. When he unrolled it on the bed, it revealed a sort of "kit" anyone could recognize. He put water and a small glob of dope in a spoon, heated it up until it bubbled. He used a cotton swab to separate the liquid from the muck as he sucked that liquid into a syringe. He flicked the syringe to get rid of bubbles.

"Why no bubbles?" I asked.

"They can kill you if you shoot them up."

"But you don't shoot up."

"Sometimes I cook for others."

"Huh," I said.

"This is pure," he declared, holding up the needle. "Someone could shoot it into their bloodstream. I only snort this quality. When you buy powder for snorting, there's all kinds of stuff mixed in."

"Uh-huh," I said.

"So, what I do with this is I squirt this into my nose. But I don't actively snort it, I let it dissolve into my nasal cavity. It takes longer to hit but the high lasts longer this way."

I watched him tilt his head back, shoot the liquid into his nose, keep his head tilted back for a bit, then slowly pull his head back up. He looked happy.

"Cool," I said. "Can I try?"

He prepared me an "extra-small" dose. As I watched him cook for me, I wasn't scared. It was only going into my nose, how bad could that be? He made it seem so hygienic. Like medicine administered by a doctor. Plus, nothing bad could happen to me when I was with Jake.

I smelled copper as the junk soaked into my nasal passage. My head filled with lead, my mouth watered, and I felt dizzy. I vomited several times. The release felt great. When I sat I felt the ocean, drifted to the bottom of it, welcomed the pressure. I felt peace, underlined by terror. Just out of reach, something horrible. But I was safe, in a quiet spell. Jake gave me bubble gum. "Sweets taste better when you're dopey," he said.

We stayed in bed for hours, which felt like days, which felt like nothing. We mumbled inaudibly while touching each other, sexlessly. Heroin didn't inspire desire; all our desires were met. Our cups were overflowing with satisfaction. Tender, cozy, wholesome feelings washed over us. We were hidden, contained, like two bears in a cave.

I lay there grasping for a feeling I thought was coming. I expected to be outraged with myself, or at least surprised. Maybe I knew I'd do it this whole time. Maybe I was one suggestion away from doing anything at all. Was that so bad? Jake cradled my head like something precious. I relaxed and opened up to the swell of beauty.

"It's cliché because it's true," I gargled.

"What is?"

"Heroin feels like jazz. Miles Davis was saying . . . when a soloist takes over, takes the story in some new direction . . . the waves . . ." I trailed off, watching my fingers held up toward the ceiling.

"Don't use that word."

"What, jazz?"

"Heroin. Only narcs use that word."

"What should I call it?"

"Nothing."

"How can I talk about it?"

"You don't."

Jake didn't want to discuss the high afterward, when we drank water and tried to pee but couldn't. It seemed like a waste not to talk about it. Every altered state was better enjoyed when reviewing it later, when building myth around it. The way all of us would go on about how drunk or stoned we were? I guess the rules didn't apply here. Dope highs go unsung. In denying the urge to gossip we gave the high more weight. Like, how you'll talk shit to your friends about a random boy you date but have trouble articulating your feelings about the one you truly love. Our relationship felt so private. We spoke our own language. Jake was a game changer. Jake and jazz and . . . *that*.

Jake didn't walk me upstairs, not even that night, when I was raw and wobbly. He never got out of his car. Well, a couple of times he had leaned against it, smoking, waiting for me to run down. But he'd never walk me to the door. My parents hadn't met him but they hated him.

I floated into bed unnoticed and dreamed of losing teeth.

SCHOOL OF THE ARTS

Three judges sat in the front row of the auditorium. The stage was empty except for a grand piano. And me. I'd never played one like that. Black and shiny, like a Jaguar. Devastating. The keys were silky ivory. They had natural, effortless weight. With a tap, they sank to my will. The pedals didn't stick and the bench didn't squeak as I swayed. A round spotlight shined on me as I blasted through the music.

My memory served me the notes on a silver platter. My hands moved on their own. I zoned out and watched myself from the outside. So small, in the gaping auditorium. So chic, in a pencil skirt (shoplifted), suit jacket (shoplifted), button-down (Mom's), argyle tights (shoplifted), and Dr. Martens Mary Janes Mom bought me for the audition. She didn't ask where my other clothes came from, she was used to me digging gems out of the PTA piles.

The drive to Winston-Salem was brutal. We woke up at six to get there in time. Mom and I chatted when we stopped at

Starbucks. About Dad and his deer and the dog. The rest of the way we listened to Prljavo Kazalište, a former Yugoslav band. She didn't try to make conversation because she knew I was too nervous to talk. Or maybe she was too nervous to.

"I can't picture you living here," she said when we pulled up to the school. It looked like something from a Bret Easton Ellis novel. Greenery and bricks and jocks with sweaters thrown over their shoulders. "Hey, y'all," I heard a dude call. It was still the South, after all.

"It's only a couple of hours away. I can come home weekends."

"You don't drive."

"I'll take the bus."

"Buses aren't safe. Why don't Americans have trains?" she asked theoretically.

"To sell cars, I think. Anyway, Jake can drive me."

"I don't like when that boy drives you. It makes me nervous."

"Okay, Mom, so I won't come home for the weekends. What do you want me to say?" She looked sad and didn't answer. So I said, "I probably won't get in."

There was no way I wasn't getting in. They worshipped me, those dusty judges. I floated through Beethoven and Bach and finished my set with Chopin. I didn't know how long the *Minute Waltz* took but my best guess was I surpassed the speed of light. A single tear dropped down my cheek as I finished. The left cheek, the one they couldn't see. I didn't do it for them or the song, I cried for myself. That tear was shed for my moment.

My hands shook as I bowed, straightened my skirt, and walked up the aisle. I heaved the double doors open to blinding light and Mom in the waiting room. She didn't notice me because her head was in her hands. I tapped her on the shoulder.

"How did it go?" she asked, eyes red.

"Perfect." I pulled her up, as if she were a fragile old lady, at forty.

"It's a cool town," she said, taking a bite of her tuna melt. We found a retro diner nearby. Not Elmo's, but I could dig it.

"Way cool." I usually took time to examine my grilled cheese. Smell it, stare at it, dip it into ketchup. This time I dug in savagely.

"I don't know if it's safe," she speculated, covering her mouth with her hand.

"What do you mean?" I crammed one half of the sandwich in my face. I felt like my late hamster, Meatball. He'd stuff his cheeks with food and save it for later. But I wasn't saving this, I was starving.

"It doesn't seem as safe as Chapel Hill."

"Thapel ill ithn't thafe," I gargled through chewed food. I hadn't eaten in days, since I'd gotten high with Jake. My stomach hadn't let me.

"What? I can't understand you."

"Nothing." I swallowed, chugged my soda, and burped.

On the way back we listened to Azra and I imagined my bright future.

THE BARN

"I didn't know you cared *this* much," Mom pleaded through the door.

"*What do you mean? I cared about this more than anything. I lived for this!*" I howled.

She sighed, picked up a plate she'd left out for me that morning, still untouched, replaced it with a new plate, and shuffled downstairs. I hadn't left my room all weekend. I was in a ball on my carpet, crying, clutching the letter. The rejection letter. *My* rejection letter.

The letter didn't tell me what I did wrong. It didn't say much of anything. Just, thanks for auditioning, but after much consideration (yeah, right) we decided to reject you and crush your dreams, blah, blah, blah. Vague, written by a robot. I read it a million times. The absence of explanation made me come up with answers myself . . . *The North Carolina School of the Arts regrets to inform you, actually we don't regret it, we hate your guts. What were you thinking? What made you believe that someone like you could get in? As soon as you left the auditorium, the judges broke down laughing. Hysterics. Everyone made fun of your audition. Your failure is the talk of the school, professors and pupils alike. They had secret cameras in the auditorium, filming the whole thing. Your humiliation is public record. They'll keep the tape in their archives for generations to come. Consider this flick your only artistic legacy. Stupid bitch.*

Did I bomb my audition without realizing? Had I been strung-out? Delusional?

There was no way to be sure, since I couldn't remember how I played. But I never remembered playing when I played well. Not remembering meant it went spectacularly. The whole point to playing well was you reached a state where your brain stopped working. No, it was something else. My grades? I had only sent them my old transcripts. They must have gotten their hands on my current stats. Was that legal? Could I sue? They shouldn't care about grades, they were an art school. They're against math and science in principle. Right? So what else could it be? My essay? No way, that was a masterpiece . . . that only left one thing. My recommendation letter. My piano teacher must have trashed me. He betrayed me. I knew he hated me but I didn't know he'd go out of his way to ruin my life on purpose. What a dick.

I'd never see him again. I'd quit piano and I'd quit everything. I wouldn't even bother hiding my new grades from Mom. I was a loser, a degenerate, a lost cause.

I heard Mom talking to someone at the door. It sounded like a boy. Like *my* boy. I heard his signature limp up the stairs, then down the hall, to my door. I couldn't believe it. He'd never even rung my doorbell before. What a prince. Mom must have been desperate to let him in.

"Kat, open up," he said.

"Go away."

"I will not."

"I'm begging you."

"I wanna see you."

"Not now!"

"I'll wait." I heard him sit down, his belts and chains clinking on the floor. "I'll have lunch," he said. I heard him pick up the plate.

"Ugh. Fine."

I reached up to open the door and fell back onto the floor.

"What's going on?" he said, hovering over me.

"I didn't get in," I cried, covering my face with my hands.

"So what?"

"So my life is over."

He sat down and rubbed my back. Then he lay down on the floor and hugged me.

I was a sucker for affection. I hugged him back and blew snot into his shirt. "What do you wanna do?"

"Die?"

"I mean tonight. Your mom says no curfew." He made an effort to use a cheerful tone. It was adorable. "She said you can stay out as long as you want as long as you come home happy."

"No way."

"Way."

"In that case . . ." I sat up and wiped my face.

"In that case?" He sat facing me.

"In that case I wanna get so high that I don't understand anything."

That night we had sex on dope. Neither of us could finish. We just kept doing it because there was nothing else to do and we were stuck in the rhythm. At one point I thought I smelled smoke but figured it was part of the high. Plus my head was in the pillow and I couldn't see anything. When I turned on my back I saw smoke behind Jake and said "There's smoke" but Jake didn't react. Smoke filled the room. "There's smoke," he said. "I told you." We moved like sloths but managed to get out of the shed with our clothes in our arms. Smoke poured out the door behind us.

"What do we do?" I asked, stunned.

"Dunno."

"Call 911?"

"Let's go." Jake walked toward the car. I stood there, watching the shed burn.

From the front of the house he yelled, "You coming?"

We fled the scene as if we started the fire ourselves. There was a sense of urgency, like we just robbed a bank. Maybe because we were high, there was an air of guilt around what happened. I knew Jake had the same thought. He raced aimlessly and his car hollered. He was shirtless and I was in my Victoria's Secret thong. The scene made me feel like a mad Gregg Araki heroine. He rolled the windows down and we laughed. Pleasure startled me, like a bucket of ice falling on my head. I kissed Jake on his hands and his arms and his neck. He parked in front of some pool hall. He said he couldn't drive with me exciting him. I was like, what are you gonna do about it? I crawled into the backseat and he followed me. I sat on top of him and went wild. Usually his feelings ruled but I didn't consider him. I'd get my kicks. When I came I was loud and didn't care that there were people around.

"You scare me sometimes," he said.

"You don't need to flatter me, you already got laid," I joked, pleased with myself.

We got dressed and went inside the pool hall. As we walked in we were greeted by tweakers and truckers in camo. They didn't bother us or ask for ID. Jake got us beer while I tried to pee, but couldn't. In the bathroom mirror I was demonic and immense. I looked deep into my eyes and watched my pupils become huge. "This is you," I said to myself, "I am you." I tried wrapping my head around the concept of myself thinking about myself. Where was Kat? Where did she live? Was I in my brain? Or my whole body? Inside my eyes? Someone knocked on the door. "Miss? You drowned in the toilet?" Jake said I'd been gone forever. We played a few rounds of pool and I won once.

The next day Mom asked why I smelled like a fireplace and after a dumb pause I said, "We went to a barbecue." Only then I grasped what had happened. If it weren't for the smell of smoke in my hair I'd swear it was a hallucination.

OPEN EYE CAFÉ

"I'm dope sick," Jake whimpered through the phone.

"But you aren't an addict." He wasn't a junkie. Just a hobbyist.

"Kat . . ." He sounded exhausted.

"You told me you can use without forming a habit?"

"Yeah, well. I used too many times."

"Whoa . . . do *I* have a habit?"

"Don't be stupid."

He said he needed my help to kick. I was to nurse him and entertain him. Dope sickness is easier with music and company. He talked about it expertly, like he'd been down this road before. He told me to pick up some things from the pharmacy and come ASAP.

"I can't drive, remember?"

"Ask your parents."

"Dad works Saturday. Mom's out doing mom stuff."

"Find a way. I'm dying here."

It wasn't a hallucination; the love shack burned down. Only two walls were left standing. It must have been the candles or the space heater or a combination of both. He lost the TV, his skateboards, and the cash he had saved in a paper bag under the mattress.

He was left with nothing. Only the outfit he wore that blazing night. A good outfit, at least. Poor Jake. He was worse off than me. I'd do whatever I could to help him. He was staying with Dexter for the moment. On the couch in the Party Room. There hadn't been a party in a while.

I took the bus downtown and walked to CVS Pharmacy. I picked up an apple, a banana, a carton of OJ, and a bottle of Pedialyte. I bought those. Meanwhile I lifted a Cover Girl powder compact, a tube of Revlon red lipstick, and a couple of trashy magazines to read while Jake slept. He warned me that he'd be "zoned out" most of the time but that he needed me to be near him regardless. "I'll feel if I'm alone."

On the way to Dexter's I stopped at Open Eye Café. I'd need black coffee to face the task ahead. Every time I went to Open Eye, which was rarely, I wondered why I didn't come more often. It was a great place to ogle cute girls who didn't shave their armpits. From the line I spotted Bob. He was in the corner, sitting on one of the moth-eaten couches. He pretended not to see me, burying his face in a comic book. The sight of him made me long for a simpler time. To think that once he was my biggest problem. I tottered over to him.

"Hey, Bob." I tapped him on the shoulder. "Hello," he said to the comic book. "Don't be afraid of me," I said.

"Who said I'm afraid of you?"

"Why won't you look at me?"

He looked at me. His eyes were angry.

"Can we forget what happened?" I offered.

"Nothing happened."

"You don't remember?"

"I remember you ran out on me like I'm some kind of creep."

"Dude. I don't mean *that*. I mean you being a dickhead about it?"

"Oh, come on. I just wanted attention."

"You're a grown man, Bob."

"Well then maybe you shouldn't be talking to me."

He went back to reading. I stood there for a minute, snorted dramatically, and stomped away. I couldn't believe he was hostile when I gave him a chance to make things right. I shouldn't have given him the chance. Doing so canceled any superiority I'd held over him. *Dammit, Kat.* I knew why I did it. Bob represented my past. I wanted to hold on to it, grab hold of him, since the present was fucked. But the past was unreachable. Like who I was freshman year was unreachable. Would I morph into a new, terrifying person each year? I couldn't fathom it. When I crossed the street I realized I left without my coffee. *At least things can't get worse.*

Dexter's Lab was spooky. The stereo buzzed Leftover Crack on minimum volume. Some bands shouldn't be played that low. Dexter was dope sick in his bed and Jake was dope sick on the couch. Ashley nursed Dexter, I nursed Jake. I belonged to a damaged family unit.

"Did our boyfriends schedule getting sick at the same time? Like preppy girls plan matching outfits?" I joked with Ashley in the kitchen. We were mixing Pedialyte cocktails.

"Laugh now . . . cry later." She looked haggard, like a mom.

"Have y'all been through this before?" I asked.

"It's nonstop. He kicks, relapses, quits, gets sick, over and over. I'm stuck dealing with it."

"That blows."

"You have no idea."

"Well, at least we get to hang out. I haven't seen you in weeks."

"Yeah, I miss you." She sighed. "I miss the mall."

"Let's go soon."

"Let's go today." She got a crazed look.

"Aren't we stuck here?"

"They're dead men," she yelled. Then she covered her mouth and lowered her voice to a whisper. "They have no sense of reality."

"What if they find out? Jake would be crushed."

"Jake won't know the difference between two minutes and two hours. When they pass out we leave. Deal?"

Jake *was* beyond reach. A human wasteland. A shell of himself. Sweaty, twitchy, agitated, irrational, unable to form cohesive thoughts. I fed him some Pedialyte and he refused to touch the fruit.

"I can't eat." He choked.

"You told me to get fruit," I insisted, shoving the apple in his face. He slapped it away and it rolled on the floor.

"Watch yourself." He moaned.

He twisted and turned endlessly on the filthy sofa, wearing only boxers. I shuddered to think how the scratchy upholstery felt against his skin. I put a sheet down for him when I arrived but within hours it was just a sweat-soaked ball of fabric pushed between his feet. He stank. He was pitiful. My heart ached at the sight of him. My maternal-girlfriend instinct throbbed with purpose. At the same time, I felt repelled.

When Jake stopped moving I took my new *People* magazine out from my bag. Just as I settled into the latest gossip, Ashley walked in.

"If we don't leave right this second I'll smother him with a pillow."

We took the bus to the mall. The moment my butt hit the seat next to hers I recognized that feeling I used to get when diving into a mosh pit: freedom. I felt like a normal teenage girl. I leaned against Ashley and she held my hand. Out of character for us both. I think she was also relieved to be away from boy problems.

When we got off the bus we were new women. Ashley squealed as she hopped into the mall. Watching her bounce around in her booty shorts and go-go boots, I gushed with admiration. I decided to start appreciating our friendship more. I needed girl time.

"Kat, where are you going?" Ashley stopped me with her arm as I was darting to the left wing of the mall. I almost slipped and did a backflip.

"Victoria's Secret. Don't we start there?"

"Let's go to Nordstrom."

"Isn't that place mad expensive?"

"We're lifting, Kat."

"I know. I mean, won't there be security?"

"We'll be fine."

I followed her into the store. She disappeared into the racks but I held back. I pretended to browse the designer fragrances. I wasn't ready to lift at Nordstrom.

Spritzing Dolly Girl, Pink Sugar, and Brit for Her kept me busy for several minutes. "I didn't know you were a Burberry girl," a voice said behind me.

I turned around to see Lucy. Her preppy friends lurked behind her. Lucy looked great. She was filled out, with some extra help from a push-up bra. Her face was glowing with youthful beauty. Her hair, which I've admired for a decade, and grown to love, as a sort of pet, was long and shiny. She styled it in mini-pigtails, so only half of her hair was pigtailed, the other half was straight and flowing. She wore Abercrombie head-to-toe . . . something she wouldn't have been caught dead in years ago. I saw her looking me over disapprovingly.

My hair was greasy and stringy. Lately I got lazy and allowed my bob to morph into a shifty mullet. A rock-and-roll mullet, but a mullet nevertheless. I was sweaty from all the walking and nursing. I couldn't recall if I had makeup on or not, but if I did, it was smeared. I wore my plaid skirt, ripped tights, Dr. Martens, and an oversized Rancid shirt I found under the passenger seat of Nosebleed's car. It was covered in cryptic stains and smelled like mold.

"Hey," I shrieked, like girls do when they haven't seen each other in a while, or hate each other, or love each other, or all of the above. "What are you doing here?"

"Shopping. What else would I be doing here?"

"Oh, duh. This mall is great, right?"

"Yep." She stared at me blankly.

Why the hell did you approach me if you aren't going to talk? I wondered.

The chore of asking questions fell on me. That was our dynamic. We used to walk to Wendy's every Saturday morning, after our weekly sleepovers. We'd eat a spicy chicken combo for lunch and talk freely, away from her parents. She'd go on about her crushes, her feelings, her problems. When I brought anything up myself she'd end up berating me. I didn't dress girly enough. *If your pants are baggy your shirt has to be tight, otherwise you look butch.* Or my personality was preventing me from being loved. *Boys don't like you because you think you're funnier than them.* Or I lacked some basic grace I was unaware of. *My mom says you're obnoxious.* I'd nod and gulp my Frosty. I realized I was better off accepting my role: the interviewer. Every friendship has the late-night host and the celebrity guest. I was her Jay Leno, she was my Charlize Theron.

"So, what's new?" I asked.

"I'm so busy. I'm on varsity field hockey and I'm packed with AP classes since I'm applying to all the good schools."

"Ouch." I offered sympathy. She had no choice but to be perfect. Her dad beat her up for Bs.

"What about you?" She grinned.

"The usual. Playing piano. Sucking at school." I pushed out a fake laugh.

"Since when do you suck at school?" She frowned.

"Since I got a boyfriend," I stated matter-of-factly, as if the two were connected.

They kind of were, in my case.

"Is it Trippy Dope?" She looked embarrassed saying the name, and resentful. She was a huge Trippy fan.

I wanted to take her hand, get on the bus, run to her house, and spend the night. I missed it. I needed it. I'd give anything to be next to her in a sleeping bag. To tell her everything. The worst parts. Then watch her fall asleep. To wake up in the morning with a friend who carried my burden with me. "He isn't my boyfriend," I muttered, unable to look at her.

"Oh, right. You sleep with people who aren't your boyfriend."

My blood rushed into my hands and feet. "What's it to you?"

"Just saying."

I'd choke on my heart if I didn't say something biting. "I know you think I'm a slut. That's why you stopped hanging out with me."

"What?" She reached a hand to her neck, like she had pearls to clutch.

"After the skate park thing, that summer."

"That's not why I stopped talking to you."

"Really."

"It didn't *help* that you screwed a bunch of skaters without telling me."

"*That's* not what happened."

"That's not the *point*. You never told me anything. You always had some secret life in the background. Like, you thought you were better than everyone else? That's shitty. You're a shitty friend."

Her specialty was throwing a grenade at your head when you least expected. My "skate park incident" spread around town that summer, in various versions, like a game of telephone. She never bothered to hear my side. How could I tell her when she didn't ask? Maybe I should have reached out to her but she was the least of my problems then. Anyway, even if I *had* done all those guys on my own, so what? She couldn't be friends with a hoe? She preferred rumors to truth. Just like everyone else. Sheep.

"I don't know what to say to that."

"You never do."

Lucy's idiotic clones tapped her on the shoulder. "Time's up," they snapped, pulling her away. Tears filled my eyes when their backs turned. I let a few drops fall and shook it off. Where was Ashley? I scanned the room for red hair. Bird-watching. Between the stilettos and platforms I spotted my cardinal. She was my best friend and partner in crime. I'd never take us for granted. I loved watching her work so I held back to see the show. She plucked a pair of Louboutins off the display and shoved them directly into her purse. Strange, considering she didn't wear sample sizes. Tall as she was, her shoe size was nine or ten, at least. Maybe she wanted them as a gift? Or a trophy?

She crept into the jewelry section, grabbed a necklace off a stand, and stuffed it in her pocket. She was never this reckless. I waved my arms to get her attention. We made eye contact and she waved back. I mouthed: *Stop*. She winked and pointed to the exit.

She always walked ahead of me so she arrived first. The instant she touched the doors, alarms blasted. That had never happened. It was the worst-case scenario. I couldn't help. She tried to run, as was protocol, but a security guard was there already, he'd been there the whole time. He grabbed her arms, looked in her purse, said something to her, and dragged her away. She didn't put up a fight. She had no chance.

Petrified, I hid behind the perfume counter, lowering myself to the ground. "Can I help you?" a lady asked. I'd hid behind the wrong side of the counter. The side where employees stand.

"Yes, ma'am." I stood up. "Can I get a sample of the uh . . ." I looked around at the bottles and called out the first one I saw.

"Channel No dot five?"

"Chanel number five? That scent's mature for your age."

"I'm mature for my age."

The lady looked at me like, *Scram, kid*. So I did. The alarms had stopped and the coast was clear. Everyone was back to minding their business, including Lucy, whom I avoided on my way out.

I walked around the mall anxiously texting Ashley. I hoped she'd reply, "I'm free. Meet at Cinnabon." Or, "I kicked that cop's ass, meet at the theater." I'd even be happy with, "I'm in jail, bail me out." She never answered. After a couple of hours I got ice cream and hopped the next bus home.

The following day I didn't hear from her or Jake. Neither of them answered me. I didn't dare call Dexter. Paranoia took over: *Ashley's in prison. Jake is dead. Or worse, they both hate you.*

I had to take my mind off my mind. All day I hung with Mom at Weaver. I brought my schoolwork and she brought hers. Mostly she read the *New Yorker* and I read a comic hidden inside my history book. She knew it was there and I knew that she knew but she didn't say anything. It was lovely, when I forgot what I was trying to forget.

Breakfast became lunch, which became dinner. "Can we stay longer?" I pleaded.

"Dad's home alone," she reminded me.

The thought of Dad sitting in his garage depressed me. He shouldn't pay for my problems. He never did anything. I was the fuckup of the family.

Later I helped Mom cook dinner (watched her cook dinner) and we all ate in front of the TV. I force-fed myself half a stuffed pepper and moved the rest of it around the plate. *The OC* was on. I couldn't tell if it was a new episode or a rerun because it was always the same: Marissa Cooper gets into trouble and everyone loves her so much that they help her out of it. Who wrote this crap? They didn't know real trouble.

After we did the dishes my parents went upstairs and I stayed on the couch with the dog. I'd sleep there that night. The smell of paws relaxed me. They've got this delicious scent, like bread baked in sunshine. I sniffed them until I had my fill, then buried my face in her fur. Trying to sleep now was like trying to meditate in the middle of a highway. In an exhausted state I decided. *Tomorrow you're going to school.*

NOSEBLEED'S

Nosebleed picked me up, as always. The only constant in my chaotic life.

"Where today? Dexter's? The shack? A café?"

"This is crazy, but I was thinking . . . school?"

"Hell yeah." He held up his hand for a high five. I missed his hand on the first try and got the second one, barely. "That was lousy," he said.

"I'm not a high-fiver."

"Clearly."

I snorted. "So what have I missed? Fill me in."

"Uhhh . . . huh?"

"What's new at school? Our crew? The hill?"

"We don't chill on the hill."

"*What?*" That was like saying the moons of Jupiter moved to Mars.

"Well, *you've* been MIA. Madeline's in the loony bin. Ashley's always at Dexter's. Charlie avoids me. Hah."

"Shit. I abandoned you."

"Nah." He shrugged but I could tell he was beat up about it.

"What do you do at lunch?"

"Go home."

"Can I come with you today?"

"Yeah. I've been holding some merch for you."

"You should have said so." I patted his leg and felt the muscles bulge as he slammed his foot on the gas.

School was . . . fabulous. I walked down the halls in slow motion. Gossip trailed me like flies on a cow. How I missed that rush. I fed my teachers various stories of my whereabouts. My math teacher was a dick but the others seemed relieved to see me.

Mountains of catch-up work and pats on my back. Exams to cram for and colleges to consider. Now that I wasn't abandoning regular school for the arts academy (shudder) I had to figure my shit out. Surprisingly, the concept elated me.

My locker combination took a few tries but I cracked it open to find surprises inside. Including a rotten apple, a bottle of chocolate milk, random trash, and photos of Trippy Dope taped everywhere. Embarrassing. I cleared it all out.

In class I cracked jokes and even the jocks laughed. I smiled brightly at each passing face in the hallway. Catching the cheerleaders walk in their flock brought me unprecedented joy. I felt a kinship with everyone. Even my teachers seemed cool. My efforts weren't one-sided. Adoration and attention followed me. Groupie Kat was back. Word on the street (in the halls) was I'd been spending quality time with Trippy on his tour bus . . . why would I burst such a gorgeous bubble?

Sure, being a delinquent had its perks. When you choose not to care about anything, nothing can hurt you. The world can't touch someone so far lost. Nobody expects a bum to pay taxes. You aren't part of society, you're beneath it, and therefore above it. My problem was, no matter how "bad" I seemed, part of me did care, so my failures hurt, even if I failed on purpose. At the beginning I thought, *Failing a test is cool if you don't try to study. It's only sad if you try and* then *fail.* But if you care even a little bit, like I did, the first version is actually sadder than the second. Because it's your fault. I was guilt-ridden. I wondered endlessly how to relieve the guilt associated with ditching, lying, and failing. It never occurred to me to simply go back to school.

At lunch Nosebleed was leaning against his car, waiting. "You ready?"

"Hell yeah." I braced myself for what he called home. A trailer, a crack house, a slum, a cardboard box, or just a bunch of newspapers and an umbrella. Nosebleed was legit, the real thing, hardest in the crew. So when he pulled up to a McMansion in a gated neighborhood near school I was like, "Are we robbing someone?"

"This is my place," he snarled.

I was used to feeling clueless about the world. Surprises didn't surprise me. My lifestyle supported ignorance and what came with it. I rejected society, and the life of a square. So anything I learned about the Life of Squares came as a rude awakening.

I want to be stereotyped
I want to be classified

I wanna be a clone
I want a suburban home, suburban home, suburban home,
suburban home

All my anthems mocked how things were. It wasn't cool to care. NO FUTURE was our motto. The less you know the better. But when *my* alternate reality surprised me? Well, I couldn't stand it. What did it mean?

Nosebleed led me through a sprawling hallway with hardwood floors, a dining room with marble columns, and into a stainless steel kitchen with one of those "island" things rich people have. I didn't say anything about his shocking wealth. I didn't want to embarrass him. It took guts to have me over. It was insulting, really, that he wouldn't hide this from me. That he wouldn't think I'd judge his "street cred" like the others would. Did he assume I didn't have street cred either?

"You wanna eat?" He opened his massive refrigerator. "We've got Hot Pockets, cold pizza, PB&J . . ."

"I'm not hungry," I said automatically.

"Me neither. Let's go to my room." Miles of hardwood and marble later we reached a staircase where he said, "Shoes off." We sat on the bottom step unlacing our boots in silence. Side by side with him on the stairs I felt like his sister, sharing this home. Going to wash up for "supper," as Americans called it. His place reminded me of one I used to frequent. I had this Christian friend. Her parents used to lecture me about communism, as if being born in a communist state made me reek of social decay. They explained, "In communism, *this* phone isn't yours. It belongs to the government." They shoved their kitchen phone in my face. They took me to church some Sundays, where I had the daylight scared out of me. Sunday school, for kids, was nothing but tales of damnation.

Meanwhile, my friend was a secret freak, masturbating with an electric toothbrush as we'd watch HBO's *Real Sex* on mute. She had to answer every thing her parents said with "Yes, sir" or "Yes, ma'am." Once, we were skateboarding at my place and she fell and hit her forehead. She bled all over her shirt, her face, her hands. It was gnarly. My parents wanted to call her parents, but she pleaded, "Please don't, they'll kill me." She cried more about "ruining her dad's dinner" than she did about the cut. When we turned twelve she moved to Germany. Poor little army brat.

Watching Nosebleed's bondage pants tread up the stairs in contrast to everything around us deemed his outfit ridiculous. Mine too. I resented him for that. His room was in character but too curated to be convincing. Posters hung so perfectly in line with each other that the color of his walls was a mystery. His bed was huge and fluffy with clean linen sheets. His desk and dresser were dust-free. Hundreds of records and clothes were organized neatly. Not the typical boy's room, definitely not a punk's room.

"These are for you."

He balanced a folded pile of shirts on his hand like a pizza box. I took it from him delicately and sifted through, lifting corners. The stack held rare shirts from the Misfits, the Adicts, Crass, the Cramps, the Exploited, and some bands I didn't know. It was the best gift I'd ever received.

"Dude!" I squealed. "How come?"

"Too small for me."

"They're incredible." I beamed.

"Try them." He fell back on his bed and put his hands behind his head. I turned around and took my shirt off. While holding my chest with one hand I reached the other into the pile and pulled a shirt from the stack randomly: an original Black Flag shirt. The arms were ripped off and small holes adorned the torso. I turned back around. "Rad." He did a thumbs-up.

"So sick," I cooed.

"Try more on," he pushed.

"There's like a million of them." I pretended not to get the hint. He wanted me shirtless in his bedroom.

"Fine." He sighed. "Sit down."

Next to him on the bed I felt an energy pulling us closer. Did he feel that? A sort of heat, like what radiates from my dog's belly when she flips over and wants to be rubbed. He put his hand on my leg and I jerked it away.

"We can't do anything, even if I want to."

"Why not?"

"Because of Jake? Duh."

"Jake sucks."

"He doesn't."

"Uh, he definitely does."

"Don't be a dick." I laughed, trying to stay upbeat. *Don't go there.*

"Since Jake showed up everything sucks."

He went there. "That's not *his* fault."

"Dude? He brought the drugs. And he took you away."

"You're so dramatic. I'm right here. And everyone always did drugs."

"Not hard drugs."

"Well, as a matter of fact, Jake is kicking his habit as we speak."

"Wow, what a hero." He mocked me.

"Jeez. Sorry you feel this way." I threw my hands up.

"It's not a feeling." He said "feeling" in an annoying Valley-girl voice. Did he think I talked that way? "It's facts. Nobody hangs, we don't even go to shows anymore."

"Everyone has their own problems. You can't blame it all on one person."

"Jake is your problem."

"Jake helps me a lot, actually."

"Yeah, how?"

"I don't have to explain that to you."

"Whatever. You used to be cool."

"I'm still cool. I just . . . grew up this year."

"Hooking up with grown-ups doesn't make you grown-up."

"Jake is nineteen."

"I don't mean Jake."

My cheeks burned. "You're one to judge," I sneered.

"What does *that* mean?"

"You never even *noticed* me until I became a groupie," I huffed. I was able to throw the term around at this point, not flinching at the lie.

He shook his head. "I just thought you needed a friend."

"I'm not a charity case." I rolled my eyes.

"Don't be pissed. I was trying to be nice."

I glared at him. Nosebleed was beautiful. I'd never gotten a good gaze at him close up, in proper lighting. In the car he was always head-banging. Now he was still and I studied him. Sharp features, clear skin, a straight nose, and clever eyes. When a good-looking boy made me feel bad I became desperate for his approval. It was basic arithmetic. I pulled at his vest and brought him closer. We kissed zealously. It was the right thing to do. It would happen in some romantic comedy where two enemies end up getting married. But there was no chemistry, just performance.

He pulled away and said, "Let's go back to school."

"I'll walk," I spat.

"Don't be stupid."

"I *am* stupid . . . for coming here." I wanted to insult him but couldn't think of anything. "Why do you even have a car when you live so close to school? Who lives *this* close to school?"

He just stared at me.

I ran down the stairs, stepped into my boots, and left. My backpack was in his car, which was unlocked. In a neighborhood like his I'd leave my car unlocked, too. I marched back toward school, mortified. I'd left the new shirts at his place. At least I snagged the Black Flag.

On the way Jake called me. Finally. He'd make me feel better.

"Jake. I was so worried," I puffed, walking up the hill toward campus. "I called a million times yesterday."

"I was out of it . . . but you wouldn't know." His tone was bitter.

I brushed it off. "Well, I tried reaching you. How are you feeling?"

"Why did you leave me?" He raised his voice.

Oh, shit. "What? When?"

"Kat."

"Oh, right, you mean Saturday? I . . . had to go home. You were asleep?"

"You're lying!"

"No. I mean," I sighed. "Yeah, I went to the mall with Ashley."

"Dexter told me. She got arrested."

Uhhhh. "Yeah, it was terrible. Is she okay? Have you heard from her?"

"Only through Dexter. He's pissed at you."

"At me? *I* didn't arrest her." My tone was sarcastic. Wrong call.

"He blames you." A stab in the belly.

"How is that fair?" I scoffed.

"She wouldn't have gone without you. She was taking good care of him before you showed up."

"It was *her* idea to go to the mall!" I was panicking, stammering. "We, we needed a break. Dexter doesn't know anything."

"Dexter knows that he hates you." Another stab, in the heart.

"Are you serious?" I was spinning. "I'll go over there and explain everything."

"Don't. I'm only telling you this, *warning* you, because I love you."

"Gee, thanks." I finally made it to school. I sat on a curb to catch my breath. "If you love me so much, why didn't you defend me?"

"Because *I'm* pissed at you, too."

"What? Let me come over there. I'll make it up to you!" I insisted, then begged.

"You can't, you're banned from the Lab. And I'm stuck here, remember? I have nowhere else to go."

"Banned from the Lab?" *May as well be dead.* "Dexter's a drama queen. He'll get over it."

"I doubt it."

"I fucked up. We're fuckups! How come I'm the only one getting punished? I can name like a million times all of us fucked up."

"Leaving us for dead was *not* cool."

"For dead? Come *on*. I sat with Dexter that night he overdosed. Y'all were just sleeping this time. Jesus."

"You don't get it. I didn't believe Dexter. Because it was so *unlike you*. I couldn't imagine that you left me." Jake sounded heartbroken. He was a master manipulator and his tricks always worked on me. Usually. I was done being criticized. It was all anyone did to me lately. I needed a good comeback.

"You can't believe I went to the *mall*? I can't believe you ruined our scene!" The moment I said it I regretted it. What seemed like a power move a second ago became insane once released in the wild. Too late to take it back.

"What did you say?" His back bled from *my* stab. He had it coming.

In a moment like that you can either back down and lose or go harder and lose, with your head up. "You only brought problems to town."

"I lost my house. I'm kicking my habit. How can you be so cruel?" His voice cracked.

My heart, guts, and brain hurt but my adrenaline sealed the pain in a Ziploc bag. There's a fine line between feeling everything and feeling nothing. If I wanted to keep him I had to apologize, I knew that. But didn't know how to. I was on a roll, toward something, and had too much momentum to halt.

"I'm not cruel. I'm honest."

"Wow." Was he crying?

"Jake?" I'd fucked up, big-time. "I didn't mean it!"

"It's cool."

"Really?"

"I get it."

"Thanks. Sorry, I'm just stressed. I love you!"

"I mean, *I get it*. Go home to your parents and forget about me."

"What? Jake." I yelled at the dial tone. He'd hung up. "No!"

His phone was off when I called back. I sat on the curb in a dumb shock until the last bell. More classes missed. Fuck it. I cried until everyone busted through the doors. A sea of schoolkids filling the parking lots. I did the unthinkable. Walked to the school bus lot and got into my old ride.

Everyone on the big yellow turd noticed my comeback. They seemed perplexed and excited. But I couldn't enjoy the attention. A hole was ripped through my chest. All of my failures came up for air at once.

Everyone hates you. You're banned from Dexter's. Your boyfriend dumped you. And he doesn't even know you've kissed Josh and Nosebleed. Poor Jake. The only one who loved you, and you threw it away. You don't deserve him. You're a bad person. A goner. Lost soul. A dog without a pack. Worthless without your crew. A nobody. Is a lone punk a punk at all? You're outcast by the outcasts. Rejected by the rejects. A forlorn freak. No reason to live. Nobody wants you, not even that corny, nerdy music school for geeks. God, you fucked that up. For what? After all this you're just heartbroken, forsaken, and flunking. At least you're still popular at school. Hah. As if that matters.

Unless . . .

That's it.

I had an epiphany and kicked the back of the seat in front of me. Carlos (the scary kid who always sat in front of me) spun around.

"What's your problem, bitch?"

"I saw a spider."

"Puta loca," he muttered.

Yes. I was obscenely popular.

I had misread my whole situation. Mistreated my circumstances. Rejected a gift from the universe. Instead of running into the arms of fate I ran away and into bad company. A once-in-a-lifetime opportunity landed in my lap and I buried it in the dirt. I held something others wanted. Limitless power could be mine. How exhilarating. A new purpose to live. My new life would begin immediately. I had to yell at the driver "That's my stop" when she drove past it. "Sorry, kid, haven't seen you in a while," she said.

It's not the last you'll see of me, bitch.

I jumped off the bus, stumbled to the ground, and dashed home.

My feet nearly fell out of my boots, which I hadn't tied since fleeing Nosebleed's. In his bedroom I had been a different person. My priorities totally mangled by my small-mindedness. I kicked my shoes off at the door and they flung in opposite directions. One almost hit my dog in the head. She took it as a playful invitation for fetch. With my boot in her jowls, she followed me to the kitchen.

I microwaved hot chocolate and made the call I'd been dreading. His info had been taped to our fridge for years. I blew on the hot chocolate while it rang. *Pick up, dipshit.*

"Durham music, this is Thomas."

"Hey. It's Kat."

"She's alive." He sounded jolly, like Santa.

"Barely."

"Your mom said you've been sick?"

"Sick of piano."

"I see . . . so the audition . . . didn't go well?"

"The audition went great. But I didn't get in. Because *you* wrote me a crappy recommendation letter."

"Hah. Did you read it?"

"No."

"So how do you know it was crappy?"

"Because I didn't get in."

"Do you think there could possibly be other reasons for that?"

"*No*, *I* was amazing. My essay was, too."

"What about your grades?"

I sipped the cocoa and burned my tongue. "Ouch. What about them?"

"Your mom says you're failing school."

"What." This jolted me. I placed my hot chocolate on the counter so as not to spill it. "How does she know?"

"Moms know everything."

"I'm going to hang up on you."

"Okay. See you Saturday?"

"Yes." I slammed the receiver down. "Ugh." I screamed and pounded the counter. I wasn't as slick as I thought. What a day of rude realizations. "Fuck." My dog jumped up and put her legs on my waist. "Don't worry, I'm not talking to you." I petted her head. She licked my knee. I fed her a treat and made myself grilled cheese.

UNIVERSITY MALL

Infatuation, ecstasy, bliss, boredom, revulsion, rebellion, rejection, regret. Those are the phases of a relationship. I decided this after ruminating on what happened with Jake.

Without a social life or love life I had time to think. I did my best thinking while watching my favorite cartoons. Looking back on what I grew up with, my problems made sense.

Looney Tunes are packed with self-destructive characters who literally blow themselves up over and over again, never learning their lesson. Or maybe they want to die. But no matter how many times they set off firecrackers or drop anvils on their heads they're stuck in another meaningless day. Endless, brutal, Technicolor chaos. Wile E. Coyote's lifestyle inspired mine. Bugs Bunny taught the art of mischief. Daffy Duck installed disobedience in my psyche. I hated Elmer Fudd, so I hated authority.

All Dogs Go to Heaven ruined any chance of my having a healthy relationship. My first crush was Charlie, the hustling alpha dog who uses the little orphan girl to make cash. Oh, the romance of being exploited by a furry scumbag. I longed for such a relationship.

Jake and Josh were dogs but they weren't Charlie.

Speaking of dogs, *Scooby-Doo* provided my second crush: Shaggy. A pothead who lives in a van. I was destined to be depraved.

"Can I help you?"

Some pimply waiter finally noticed me.

"Thank God. I thought I was invisible."

"Excuse me?"

"Never mind. Y'all have a piano player?" I pointed to the baby grand in the back of the dining room.

"Sometimes."

"Got any spots available?"

"Perhaps."

"I could play weekends."

"Um, we'd have to hear you first."

"Well, duh."

He glared at me. He hated me. Who didn't?

"I'll bring the manager," he mumbled.

Southern Season was a gourmet grocery and restaurant in University Mall. It had an impressive selection of fancy candy, imported wine, and shiny kitchen tools for deranged housewives. It was the only place in the state where you could cop Kinder eggs.

The restaurant had a café, which was cute in a Parisian way. Yeah, I'd seen in *Passport to Paris* with the Olsen twins. Recently I'd spent lots of time there, reading magazines while waiting for

Jake. Late in our relationship I avoided waiting for him to pick me up from home. My parents would complain that he was late or that he looked weird. "Is he in a gang?" Mom asked, eyeing his red bandanas. "No, he's in style."

University Mall was a minimall, not a megamall like Southpoint. Southern Season was the mall's main attraction. The other shops were parasites: JCPenney for soccer moms, an "eccentric" boutique for divorcées, Payless Shoes for immigrants, Bath & Body Works for sluts, Chick-fil-A for stoners, Roses for broke families, a drugstore I stole candy from, an electronics shop for dads, and a "local arts" gallery for nobody, closing any minute. The mall had a unique smell. Sterile, chemical, void. It was always empty. I could make rounds on the tiled floors and pretend I was in a mansion waiting for a forlorn beast to invite me to dinner. *Eat the gray stuff, it's delicious, don't believe me? Ask the dishes.*

University Mall was near Eastgate, a strip mall. Both were walking distance from my house—a suburban miracle. Eastgate used to have a movie theater but some developers tore it down to make a bigger movie theater. They promised. Years passed and there was just a pile of gated-off rubble in its place. A wasteland. That theater had been a favorite, Lucy and I used to go every weekend. Luckily the PTA and VisArt Video still stood strong near the rubbish. Intellectual, Gen X hotties worked there. Everyone knew the staff knew everything about films but nobody would dare ask them about one. They'd tear you apart from behind foggy glasses. I dreamed of working at VisArt but was terrified to ask for an application. If I got rejected I'd never be able to show my face there again. And then what would I do? Rent videos from Blockbuster? I wasn't that kind of girl.

Playing piano at Southern Season was my teacher's idea. Well, he never heard of Southern Season but he suggested I find a "new outlet" for my playing. He said I should learn to love piano again, without associating it with the academy, auditions, or whatever. Playing at restaurants wasn't a bad idea. I could make money. I was addicted to having new clothes and was scared to lift without Ashley. Especially after what happened to her. I did not miss shopping at the PTA.

I did miss Jake. The first few days without him I cried through a dozen rolls of toilet paper. Mom consoled me. "This will be hard but you must not give in. It will pass, do not call him." She thought I had broken up with him on purpose. I let her believe it, so she had something to be proud of. It wasn't only Jake I'd broken up with. It was Ashley, Dexter, Charlie, Nosebleed, the Lab itself. The Party Room. My people. I didn't call anybody. This was for the best. I was moving on to something better.

I would make school work for me. The kids there worshipped me. The first week back on the school bus, away from the hill, wasn't easy. Luckily, Ashley and Madeline weren't around. I imagined Madeline in a straitjacket and Ashley by Dexter's hospital bed. I rarely ran into Charlie. Nosebleed avoided me as I did him. I was slowly building a new life using my groupie identity. I was so lucky and grateful. Without my legend status I would be miserable. Destitute. Hopeless. I had the chance to start fresh.

I didn't have long to go. The semester was almost over. Prom was approaching. I just had to pass my tests, make new friends, and move on. No, I would not become desperate. I would not go emo.

"Miss?" An older gentleman came up from behind me. I never used the word *gentleman* but he was one. Southern charm and all that jazz. He smelled like cigars, musk, and whiskey. He had a full head of white hair. Silver fox. He seemed pleased with himself. If I were him, I'd be pleased, too. He was like a male Sharon Stone, in that scene in *Basic Instinct*, where she asks the cop for a cigarette and he says he doesn't smoke and she says, "Yes you do." You know how some people can be a scene in a movie?

"You're interested in playing piano for supper?"

It killed me when people said supper. "Yes." I swiveled my stool around to meet him at eye level. "I'm really good."

"We'll see about that."

He saw about that.

SOUTHERN SEASON

I wowed the silver fox and earned my supper spot. All it took was the Moonlight Sonata and some "Take the A Train" improvising. People were so easy, so gullible. Silver Fox said he'd pay me a hundred bucks to play for a couple of hours, plus a meal at the end of the show. I didn't like anything they served so I invited my piano teacher to come watch and eat on me. He seemed uneasy but I knew he wouldn't let me down.

I wore an empire waist minidress Ashley lifted for me back before she hated me.

She got it at Bebe. A store not made for me. When she stuffed it in my bag I was like, "This is cute, but not cool."

"If *you're* cool you can make *this* cool."

"I don't know if anyone is *that* cool."

I needed a second opinion. I showed it to Jake and he hated it. He was like, "That's the ugliest thing I've ever seen, don't ever wear that around me." I buried it under my lifted things, which I kept hidden in the back of my closet, in case Mom ever went nosing around.

The dress fit well but made me look brain-dead. I knew Silver Fox would approve. He made it clear that I had to dress up. "No fishnets," he'd instructed, eyeing my legs. Mom was so excited for my debut but I didn't invite her. What if my piano teacher and I clicked? What if he kissed me?

The dining room was packed with yuppies. They watched me walk in and studied how I sat at the piano. We had a mutual understanding. I felt what they wanted and served it to them, in return for their undivided attention. They clinked their silverware quietly as I led them into fantasy. I was their teen dream. Pure potential. Small-town legend, on the brink of discovery. I was who they'd wanted to be. Who they could have been, had they not saved themselves for marriage. Had they studied abroad, started painting, been free. I was who they were when they dreamed. My piano teacher was missing. I blamed his wife. Still, without him, the night was a victory. Maybe better, even. Around him I had no confidence. Free of authority I could fly.

After my set I took the money, refused their food, and cruised the mall. I treated myself to magazines. In the drugstore I copped *Vogue*, *Elle*, *People*, and *Rolling Stone* . . . Trippy was on the cover. It said, "Rock & Roll Comes Out." Comes out of what?

I sat on the curb outside the mall to read the profile. My heart pounded as my brain computed the words:

"Think you know Trippy Dope? Think again. You know him as a macho rock star . . . what if we told you he's also a gay icon?

I gasped.

"Poolside at the Chateau Marmont, Trippy Dope confessed exclusively to Rolling Stone, *'I'm sick of hiding. Tired of lying. I wanna live my life. All my flings and girlfriends were fake, even the famous ones. The womanizing rocker thing was a shtick. The whole, I'm the next Mick Jagger, I'll fuck any chick, the younger the better, blah, blah, blah—that got embarrassing. Honestly, I'm more ashamed of portraying a sexist stereotype, than anything . . . The truth* IS *rock and roll and if you can't handle it? Maybe you aren't as hip as you thought.' So, reader, are you hip?"*

The piece dished it all. Trippy was brave and his path toward truth was a triumph. The pictures accompanying the profile revealed a new man. He was shirtless and barefoot as always but his face changed. Once tortured, twisted, and grim, his grin shone bright. His eyes were wide with relief. As a fan, I was happy for him. As the *girl* pretending to be the *groupie* who had an *affair* with him? This wasn't good. I could hear them already . . .

"What's worse than a poseur?"
"A fraud."

"She fucks gay dudes?"
"No, don't you get it? She didn't fuck Trip in the first place."

"The whole thing was bogus."
"She's a liar."
"And a virgin."

"And a loser, most of all."

"Let's throw stones!"

"She'll die a poseur!"

The punks who weren't already against me would surely turn on me for this. I was a target for the normies, too. If they read *Gunshot* you can bet your balls they read *Rolling Stone*. Nobody was safe now. I was spit on the sidewalk.

I had to ditch town. Flee the state, the country, the world. Could I hop a train to another universe? I wished the planet would get destroyed like in *The Hitchhiker's Guide to the Galaxy*. I didn't even care if I would be able to hitchhike to safety. Getting blasted into oblivion was fine. I didn't have a towel with me anyway. *Don't panic. Yeah, right.*

I only had one person to turn to.

I threw the magazines in the trash and dashed home.

"How did it go?" Mom asked hopefully.

"Not now, Mom." I disappeared into my room.

Holding back spontaneous combustion, I typed a desperate email.

Dear Sabrina,

It's Kat. From the Cat's Cradle. Remember me? I was backstage at Trippy Dope's show. You wrote that article and published pictures of me sitting on his lap. You declared me a groupie. It took over my life. I had to pretend to be some wanton star-fucker, which, as you know, isn't true. (No, I couldn't tell the truth. Who wants to admit to being less cool than people think they are, suddenly?? Ugh.) That wasn't your intention, I guess, but it happened. And now this bombshell's out, that HE came out. So MY truth is out. After I spent months bullshitting. (You have no idea what I went through for that.) And it was all for nothing. Because now all my friends will hate me. They hated me before the latest news but it won't help, obviously. My life sucks. And I don't know what to do. So I thought I'd write to you. That's all.

Kat ^. _ .^

PS: Your email address is all over your website, I'm not a stalker or whatever.

She replied instantly.

Darling Kat,

I'm glad you reached out. I'd say sorry but there's nothing to be sorry about.

Press is press and all publicity is good publicity. Feelings get hurt. It's part of the game. Honestly, I thought I did you a favor. Like, HELLO! I made you the center of attention? A local celebrity? Anyway, I get it. The pressure. I didn't mean any harm. I was doing my job . . . and trying to maintain Trip's reputation (something he insisted, at the time). That being said, whatever problems you've encountered as a result of a gossip piece aren't my fault. It sounds like the fault of your small town and the small-minded people in it. What are you doing there? You seem cool. Come visit me! My phone number and address are below, hit me up if you're ever in the city.

XO
Sabrina

PS: Nobody here remembers you or that dumb story.

I knew what to do. My heart wasn't up for it but I had no alternative. He was my only hope, my Jedi. I texted Jake with shaking hands.

"I kno U h8 me but if U drive us 2 NYC we have place 2 crash."

He called because he didn't like texting. It took too long, in his opinion, having to press a single key several times to get the right letter. I'd memorized which numbers became which letters pressed which times. Jake said he'd start texting when they made phones with full keyboards on them. Fat chance.

"Why haven't you called?" he clipped.

"What? I . . . thought you don't want to talk to me?"

"Why wouldn't I?"

"Because we broke up?"

"Did we?"

"Are you serious? I've been in mourning."

"I've been on this couch. I'm sick of it."

"So . . . you'll drive us to New York?"

"I'll drive us wherever."

That night I packed my backpack, but not how I'd packed it for Josh.

I shivered at the thought of him. If only he'd shown up to the Cave . . . I'd be long gone already. But there was no time for self-pity. This time, I packed my favorite looks. My plaid skirt, fishnets, concert shirts, Victoria's Secret thongs, and Cover Girl makeup. My laptop, too. I'd wear Dad's moto jacket, boots, and jeans on the way, in case it was cold. Movies in New York always put people in scarves. I considered leaving a note for my parents but figured it was best to figure out the lie once I got there. Once it was too late.

Jake showed up in the morning while my parents were walking the dog. Being hugged by him that day was like being wrapped in a fluffy blanket after falling asleep in the snow. Sniffing his hoodie hit the spot. His beauty dazed me. He seemed normal, healthy. The couch did him good. He had a flower, plucked from someone's yard, the roots still clinging. His other hand held a square wrapped in newspaper. I tore it open to reveal a burned CD, with tracks penned on it. A mix tape was the ultimate show of love. The selection was fantastic. "Nightclubbing" by Iggy Pop, "Atomic" by Blondie, "Sing" by Blur, "Perfect Day" by Lou Reed . . . I was floored. You know how much energy a good mix took? We listened to it in the car.

"I missed you," he said, putting his hand on my leg.

"I missed *you*." I grabbed his hand and kissed it. "I've been so sad, Jake. I thought it was over."

"Nah. It was just . . . a bad time. You hurt me."

"I love you. I'll never hurt you."

"One thing has nothing to do with the other."

Jake was so wise, so deep, so gorgeous. How did I survive a whole week without him? I texted Mom, "Lucy picked me up 4 surprise sleepover." And turned my phone off.

Yes, I felt guilty. But at the end of the day, you're either an asshole or a sucker. When you expect others to treat you the way you'd treat them, or think you would, if things were reversed, which they never are, that's the ultimate sucker move. We never are in each other's places. Every place is unique, uniquely bad. Only a sucker wastes time thinking about trading places and not paying attention to what's really going on. The assholes always win because they're the ones who don't stress. Stress kills, you know.

We listened to the mix CD and held hands for hours. We stopped at a gas station to pee and get gas. We didn't stop at any diners because we had so long to go. I didn't ask about Ashley or Dexter. They were history.

"I'm beat,." Jake grumbled. "Can you drive?"

"I don't have a license."

"Why not?"

"I dunno. I ride the bus or have other people drive me."

"Yeah, but if you had a license now it would help me."

"Well, sorry. I didn't plan on randomly driving to New York without telling my parents."

"Do you know how?"

"Well, yeah. I was practically brought up in a garage. Dad taught me in parking lots. So that I'd know in case of an emergency."

"This is an emergency."

"Jake, even if I *could* drive, I don't know where to go. I can't read maps."

"You can do it. I'll tell you how."

"No, Jake."

"Fine, then we'll crash because I'll pass out at the wheel."

"Let's stop at a motel."

"I'm broke."

"I've got like eighty bucks, from a piano gig."

"So we spend it all on a motel and then what?"

"I don't know."

"You didn't think this through."

"No, I didn't think through disappearing to New York."

"Don't freak out."

"I'm not freaking out!" I screamed.

Jake parked off an exit and told me the way. "Just follow the signs. You stay on I-Ninety-Five North for another few hours. Don't go off somewhere else. Eventually you reach the exit for the tunnel. The exit is Fourteen, for I-Seventy-Eight East. You can wake me up then."

"How long will it take?"

"I don't know, a couple of hours? We're almost in Philly."

He coached me as I merged back onto the highway. I felt like Dionne in that scene from *Clueless*. But I didn't lose my shit like she did. I stayed calm. Maybe I had more of my dad in me than I thought.

When I looked over, he was out cold. I kept my eyes on the cars in front of me. Their lights led me. Driving isn't hard if you stay in your lane and watch the signs. Driving isn't hard if you don't think about all the idiots around who could maul you any second. It's not hard if you don't think about how you could crash with one wrong move. Kill Jake in his sleep. Driving isn't hard, not if you don't think about where you're going, with whom, and why. It's easy, practically, if you don't consider your parents sitting at home, wondering about you. Driving is the best, when you accept you have no future.

If you asked me I wouldn't know what to tell you. How did I make it to New York? I followed the cars that were going to New York. How did I know they were going to New York? I just did. By the time I saw the skyline I wanted to keep it for myself. I didn't break Jake's sleep until we were in the city that never sleeps. It was dark. My back was drenched with sweat. My hands looked like they'd been immersed in a bathtub for hours. My eyes were popping out of my head.

"Wow, you did it." Jake stretched.

"I had no choice."

"So, where does this chick live?"

"Oh, right." I hadn't told Sabrina we were coming. A small detail I forgot. I didn't even write her info down before getting in the car. They were in my email. Thank God I brought my laptop. "We need to find Wi-Fi."

SABRINA'S

I checked my email in a fluorescent internet café and called Sabrina through Jake's phone. I was afraid to turn my phone on. Sabrina wasn't mad that I rang her out of nowhere or that I showed up unannounced. She was like, "So fun! I'm having a party, bring booze, you can crash on the couch if nobody claims it for sex." She lived downtown on Allen Street.

"She's *here*!" Sabrina announced on my arrival. She was wearing a hot-pink minidress and yellow cowboy boots. She hugged me hard and smelled like candy. The same scent that jolted me backstage. "Guys, this is *Kat*. She's this kid I met in North Carolina, with Trippy, I mean, never mind"—she winked at me, like, *Your secret is safe with me*, then continued—"Anyway, that's irrelevant, she's *so cool*. Kat. This is Jimmy. Jimmy is a painter. That one over there is Julian . . . Casablancas, you know him, right? Haha. Okay, this is my intern, Jemma, ignore her. There's Lena, she's rich and just hangs around. I guess she's a socialite? Emily is a writer, Rachel is a poet but also an escort, Matthew is an artist, there's some shaman, and his boyfriend, and a bunch of random people I don't know."

Nobody looked at me, which was a relief. I introduced Sabrina to Jake, who was randomly polite. He stood up straight and acted like an adult. Seeing him change his demeanor to impress someone was unsettling and unattractive. We didn't bring any booze because we were underage but Jake told Sabrina he would pitch in cash (my cash, no doubt) if anyone made a beer run.

Sabrina's apartment was tiny and wonderful. It looked lived-in, like it had a long, sordid history. Her closet was packed full of wild coats. Gorgeous shoes were lined up on the floor. Her bedroom was sparse but sexy. Her bed was the centerpiece, accessorized by succulents and paintings. There was another bedroom next to the bathroom, which remained locked. Mostly everyone hung out in the kitchen. There was a fat couch and a tiled floor fit for dancing.

Sabrina's guests were in their twenties, a few maybe thirty. None of them were punk but they were cool. They wore skinny jeans and leather jackets (plain leather, no patches or studs). Their bodies were strung-out, their hair was shaggy, and their attitudes were aloof. If I had to guess I'd say they were indie rock, post–glam rock, or . . . something new, something that other places hadn't picked up on yet. I avoided Julian Casablancas, I didn't want to put myself in another trap. After all, we had beef. He'd given me the bad advice to "roll with it" back at home.

Jake went to the fire escape to talk to some guy in head-to-toe denim. Denim bummed Jake a cigarette and after the smoke they went to the bathroom. I stuck to Sabrina and observed her lead conversations I didn't get. She spoke passionately about things I'd never heard of and people I'd never met. Her friends tossed off references I couldn't place and bounced around names I didn't know. I nodded and laughed on cue.

Jake hugged me from behind and whispered, "I've gotta bounce for a bit."

"Where are you going?" I turned to look at him.

"Just getting some air," he lied.

"We're gonna score," Denim confessed.

"Fine." I shrugged. They left in a hurry.

"Kat. Change the music!" Sabrina barked.

I took the CD out of my backpack and threw it in her boom box. The familiar sounds lifted my mood. I danced in her kitchen and chugged liquor from various bottles. I wanted to feel like what I was acting like I felt, but couldn't quite reach it. It was like squinting to see clearly. Part of me was somewhere else.

"I love this album!" Sabrina squealed.

"My boyfriend made it for me!" I bounced.

She laughed. "*No* he didn't."

"Yeah, he did." I was panting, sweating.

"He *said* he made this for you?"

"Yep."

"Oh, babe. I'm so sorry."

"What?"

She put her hands on my shoulders to make me stand still. "This isn't a mix. This is a soundtrack."

"That's impossible. He made this for me *today*."

"This is the *Trainspotting* soundtrack. I've got a copy of it." She went into her bedroom and fetched the CD. I read the tracks and they were the same.

Jake was a poseur. I was devastated.

"How you doing, kid?" Sabrina asked. I must have looked troubled.

"I've got that teenage depression," I quoted Eddie and the Hot Rods.

"Huh?"

"I'm in a weird moment."

"Growing up is hard." She tossed me a look and I held on to it for comfort.

"All I wanted was to be cool. When I became cool I didn't know what I wanted."

"I used to want to be cool. Now I want to be powerful. You'll see, the things that make kids cool are the same things that make adults *uncool*."

"I guess that makes sense."

"You're quite impulsive, I see. The thing about impulsivity is, for it to really have meaning, it requires follow-through."

She left me with that and went to throw up in the toilet.

I sat on the couch in the kitchen and watched people have fun, like I used to do at Dexter's Lab. Chapel Hill felt far away, like it didn't exist. But that didn't provide relief. It only made me feel hollow. Like everything I'd done up until that point was irrelevant. Eventually everyone left, Sabrina put on pajamas and left me alone on the couch.

I pretended to be asleep as Jake let himself in. He lay next to me and started snoring. I couldn't wind down. I counted the items in Sabrina's kitchen until sunrise. Then I showered, brushed my teeth with my finger (I'd forgotten to pack my toothbrush), and snuck out with my backpack.

The streets were dirty and steamy. The sky was hazy and low. People were coming home from parties and others were going to work. So many people living full lives I knew nothing about. All their problems mattered to them tremendously. And I was nobody. The size of the city overwhelmed me. I tackled it practically. I pictured each street as a single Franklin Street. New York City is just a bunch of small towns' downtowns, mashed together. The city is organized in a grid, easy to follow. One street at a time can't beat you . . .

That trick worked for a few blocks. Then truth hit me, irreversibly. The infinite possibilities of infinite streets made me feel tiny, but I'd rather be obscure than obsolete.

PEARL DINER

I made a pilgrimage by asking people for directions. I tried to come off like a new college student, rather than a tourist, or whatever I was. Everybody I approached seemed annoyed but not necessarily at me.

First I hit the Bowery and found CBGB. Where it all happened. I tried to grasp what went down around me. I recalled the names and dates like I was studying for an exam. The Ramones were discovered there. Television, the New York Dolls, the Velvet Underground, Patti Smith (whom I never liked, for some reason), and Blondie, they all played at CBGB's. They got fucked up there and fucked each other there. Richard Hell and Iggy Pop, the bad boys of history, broke countless hearts inside those walls.

Overdoses and strokes of genius took place in the bathroom. It was the birthplace of punk, the womb. English bands copied what was going down in CBGB's and did a better job marketing it—anyone who tells you otherwise is a poseur.

I tried to channel their energy, but I couldn't reach it. *That* energy lived in another time. It was over. The time I lived in was pointless. Harsh reality. Joey Ramone didn't swoop in to save me. Debbie Harry was nowhere in sight. The glory days were over before I was born. The truth was I was alone. Just some kid standing around on an ugly street next to a closed venue. I wore sweaty, wrinkled, slept-in clothes and a heavy backpack. I fit in with the homeless dudes hanging around. No magic door opened up for us. It's like they say, "You just had to be there," not visit the graveyard afterward.

I toured the East Village. The legendary punk neighborhood. St. Marks was all hookah bars, gift shops, and restaurants. Maybe it was too early in the day for punk rockers. I passed Search and Destroy and Trash, two iconic punk shops. They weren't open yet.

I wanted to hit Fifty-Third and Third in honor of the trick-turning track but did the math and figured it would take all day to walk there. I wasn't in the mood to get lost on the subway or overpay for a cab. Could I find Max's Kansas City? Was that still around? I got lost and eventually made it to Chinatown. My favorite part so far, aside from all the dead animals hanging in windows. Their corpses led me to the financial district. I assumed, via the suits. There I found a diner. The Pearl.

You could always depend on a diner. No matter where you found yourself in America, a diner was a diner. It offered familiar foods at familiar prices. If you avoided local specialties, daily specials, complicated dishes, or fish—and ordered a *usual*, you'd never be disappointed. I asked for my grilled cheese with extra cheese, extra coleslaw, and extra pickles on the side. And black coffee and Diet Coke.

I sat back in the booth and closed my eyes. This school year was shot. I thought about the next one. I could still get my shit together. I'd try out for jazz band. There was no way I wouldn't get into jazz band . . . jazz band was full of suckers. I'd make a hundred bucks a week and save up for something life-altering. I'd get my grades up and be good to my mom. I'd stop lying. I'd break up with Jake, for good. I'd get my driver's license.

A waitress brought my plate. She was a few years older than me, with bleached hair piled on her head, bloody lipstick, and jade eye shadow. Her winged eyeliner reached her eyebrows, which were plucked into check marks. She wore white tights and high heels with her uniform, which clung to her. She hummed to herself, like she was onto something nobody else knew. I wanted to be her. She set my plate down with a wink and strutted off.

As I watched her wiggle away it hit me that she was the only person who knew where I was. At that moment, nobody from my life could find me. There was no way for them to track me down, not unless I called or answered their calls. If I didn't reach out to them, they couldn't get me. I thought, *So this is what it's like for Josh*. I felt the world swell around me and swallow me up.

I could disappear.

The sight of the sandwich repulsed me. I pushed the plate away, chugged some coffee, and left cash on the table. Then I walked outside for a slice of pizza.

ACKNOWLEDGMENTS

I'd like to thank all the bands in this book. Your music made me feel like a main character even when I was just sitting around a gas station parking lot. The Cat's Cradle—you made us proud to grow up in North Carolina. Thanks to the "Post Office Punks." The character Josh is based on a real boy who isn't with us anymore. Thank you, Josh, we won't forget you. The late, great Giancarlo DiTrapano took initial interest in this manuscript and guided me. His wisdom continues to shine down on us. My fabulous agent, Maria Whelan, and brilliant publisher, Tracy Carns, are New York legends and I'm so proud to work with them. Thanks to all the people who inspired characters in this book. My piano teacher, Tyson. Stefano and Winkle, you changed my life and make me so happy every day. I love you. *Hvala, Mama, Tata, i Ana. Volim vas.*